Undress for me . . .

teasing HANDS

ELENA M. REYES

Cover: Elena M. Reyes
Editors: Marti Lynch

Original Publication Date: October 7th, 2015

Re-Release: January 3rd, 2019

Genre: FICTION/Romance/Erotica

Summary:

The hands kneading my flesh into submission are strong, yet gentle. Rough, yet tender. His talented fingers dig deep into my naked flesh, applying the perfect amount of pressure, bending me to his will.

His will that now entices and burns itself into my every pore—ruins me. Once a stubborn and independent woman, I find myself wanting to give him all that I am and power over everything I can be under his guidance.

Camden Daniels has a voice full of sin built to destroy my mental walls. The gravelly timbre of his tone controls my resolve with a single utterance from his lips:

"Undress for me."

Contents

Acknowledgments

These books are dedicated to my readers and friends.
To those that make me laugh when I get frustrated. To those that love my characters as much as I do. To those that send me messages of encouragement, and share my work with others, simply because they're passionate about my books.
To all those people I say; thank you.

Prologue

AMANDA

"Undress for me."

That was all he said. No preamble or false pretense concerning what we were—I was—here for. It was all for pleasure. A fuck. He would never offer me more than that.

The sad part was that I craved that elusive even more: a relationship with all the benefits that came with being owned by Camden. Too bad for me, it would never come to be, and that was a reality I'd come to accept. Decisions had been made.

With a small nod, I acknowledged his command, then disrobed before him. A shot of melancholy raced through me while the standard-issue spa robe fell to my feet. Today would be the last time I entered this room and served my body to him. No longer would his hands squeeze and mold my pliant flesh.

My heart stuttered at that thought. Was he going to let me leave this room as just another client, the session having come to an end? Or would he stop me?

Camden's feet came into view, bare and perfect. Just like the rest of him. My gaze traveled upward to the soft white linen pants he wore whenever I was in his space. They were threadbare, almost nonexistent, and indecent. The sweetest of tortures for me. His cock was thick and hard, pressing at the thin fabric and doing nothing to hide his size or the drops of liquid visibly seeping through the engorged head of his shaft. It twitched under the heat of my gaze, and I licked my lips. How could he be so beautiful? Be everything I never knew I wanted, but now desperately needed?

He isn't yours.

Those three words brought things back into perspective. I would be strong. Had to be—

"Look at me." His voice; fuck him and the things they did to me. *"Please, gatita."* My eyes snapped up and met his, which looked tortured and desperate. "I need you here with me, not miles away. You know the rules."

Rules. Funny.

The snort that escaped me wasn't cute. It wasn't meant to be. "Which rules are you referring to? The ones that protect you from loving me?"

"Amanda, please. Let's not ruin our time—"

I ignored his bullshit and continued to push. "Or are you referring to the ones that make me feel like nothing but a dirty little secret? Like I'm your whore?"

Camden's nostrils flared, and his fists clenched at his sides. "Don't you ever fucking—"

"Or what?" I laughed bitterly. There was no going back for us.

"Fuck, little girl." He growled and reached out to grab my arm, but I was quicker and pulled back.

I moved until my back hit the wall; the space between us gave me just enough breathing room to get my point across. "Don't," I begged. My voice was hoarse from having to keep my emotions under control. "Don't feed me your lies or excuses. It is what it is. I'm the client and you, my masseuse. Just do what you're being paid to do."

"What the fuck is wrong with you?" Camden stalked forward, lithe, like a jungle cat trapping his prey. "Is this because of what happened at Rage?" I didn't answer and looked away. Seeing him there, with *her* of all people, had crushed me. "You know nothing happened, *gatita*. I would've told you if it had." He caged me in then, hands on the wall to either side of my head. There was no escaping his perfection when he was this close. "You can't go all jealous on me and throw a tantrum when I don't belong to you."

His words stung, yet they were just what I'd come to expect from him. What I needed to hear to cut the emotional ties that held me his captive. "That goes both ways, you know?"

"What's that supposed to mean?" The rumble in his chest made my knees feel weak.

"Exactly what it states. I am not yours to hold onto anymore."

Camden banged his fist once against the wall before pulling away. He was too possessive of what he didn't want to own.

"Amanda…I can't—"

"Neither can I," I interjected in a remorseful whisper, then pulled myself off the wall.

My feet carried me over to the bed in the center of the room, but before I laid down on the cold surface, I walked over to my purse and pulled out a pair of panties. It wasn't much in the way of coverage, but my point had been made clear. Camden's normally clear blue eyes were stormy, flickering from mine to my legs, and the physical representation of the invisible wall I was erecting between us. He stayed silent as he stared at me. It was better this way. Hurt less.

Lying down, I grabbed the plain white sheet he kept for show on the small table next to the bed and pulled it over my lower half. The weight of his stare made my movements jerky. Thick tension surrounded me. His eyes burned me.

"There's somewhere I need to be within the next hour." My low tone was like a loud wail inside the small sanctuary, a room where opulence and soothing music played in the background. This space was meant to be warm, relaxing, and what others used to forget their worldly troubles. To let go.

For me, though, it was a different kind of release that came with each session. I now yearned for what his fingers could make me do. The way he tore pleasure from my body without asking permission. None was ever needed. Camden conquered and dominated my body.

Only he could give me what I craved, both mentally and physically. The way those masterful hands rubbed and extricated my troubles, attracting my naturally submissive sensuality to come forward and play, was all Camden.

His hand reached out and grabbed the sheet covering me. He fisted the thin material in his hands but didn't touch me, and I felt the scorching waves of heat which rolled off his body.

"Where do you have to be, Amanda?" His question came out as a low rumble, animalistic and hypnotic. "It's off-season, and you don't have practice."

I shrugged and closed my eyes. "None of your business."

"The fuck it isn't," he all but snarled and pulled the sheet from my body. "Where the hell are you going?"

"To finally move on." They were the wrong choice of words; I knew they would be the moment they passed my lips.

"Never."

One word was all he gave me before his hands flipped me over and his mouth took possession of mine. Camden's kiss told me everything he couldn't.

That I was his.

He wasn't letting me go.

It also said he knew I was aware of his ownership over my person. The same way he acknowledged my submission to his male dominance. There was no other person for either of us, yet he wouldn't give in to me.

Sadly, between his bullshit excuses and client non-fraternization rules, all I would ever be was Amanda Brooks to him. The daughter of a city council member, a women's college basketball player, and a client.

It killed me to accept what had been plain to see, when all I wanted was to forever be his sweet little *gatita*.

ONE

Amanda

You got this. It's just you and the net. Right now, you're outside your house practicing. No pressure. You got this.

The crowd was on its feet as the final minutes in the game wound down. We were dominating, destroying our opponent's defense, and exposing their weakness to every fan who watched from the stands.

It felt good. *Too good.* The inner bitch in me wanted to gloat in front of their angry faces while they tried to block me inside the paint. Screw that. The women of Florida State simply had no answer for the united power house that was the University of Miami. Their team was more focused on the greatness of one player than the unstoppable force of a whole unit working together.

The cacophonous stomping of feet reverberated throughout the stands and shook the gymnasium. The UM fans were loud; the buzzer hadn't even gone off and already they were celebrating the newest addition to the school's trophy case.

The united chant of: "*Let's go, Canes!*" filled the gymnasium. It pulsed through me—pumped me up with pure adrenaline while I got ready for the last play of the night.

"Amanda!" Coached yelled out, and I looked over. He made the signal for a time-out, but I shook my head. That would only give them time to counterattack if I missed. This way, if push came to shove, we would head into overtime.

All we needed was one more basket, and the trophy was ours.

"End this shit," Jennifer, our center, shouted over the roar of the crowd. She passed by me, leaving her post near the rim to push away the two players guarding me. It worked, and the opening I needed was created.

Right outside the three-point line.

The ball landed in my hands with just under seventeen seconds left on the clock. The pass was rapid, almost too fast for the other team to follow. Courtney, my best friend and forward, smirked then did her signature two-finger hand wave.

"You got this," she shouted then blocked the other team's point guard from getting in my way. The sound of the seconds ticking away was loud while that final buzzer wound close.

My brows scrunched in concentration; the entire school's basketball season rested on my shoulders. Right. No pressure.

After taking one more glance at the clock, I made my move. The ball hit the floor and the room grew quiet. My hand manipulated the ball. It bounced rapidly once, twice—my arms rose up, my wrist tilted back, and before I could blink, all I heard was the *swoosh* of the net.

Just like that, we were champions. It was a high the likes of which I've never felt before. The screams and uproar that came from the stands was overwhelming. Deafening. The band began to play, and my legs were swept out from under me when I was placed upon my teammates' shoulders.

I didn't spare the other team a second glance.

Gatorade coolers were being picked up and tipped over the coaching staff's shoulders. Everyone rushed onto the gym's floor. We were soaked and not giving a crap.

"We're champions, baby!" Courtney yelled and wrapped her slender arms around my shoulders the moment I was put down.

We squealed and laughed. Best feeling in the world. Nothing would ever compare.

"You know they are waiting?" I shuddered and turned to look over at the stands. *They* were where I knew they'd be. Proud mothers were the worst in moments like these. At least ours were.

She looked at the waving socialites and cringed. "We'll be showcased like prized stallions."

"We could just head back and escape with one of the girls. Or Coach," I deadpanned, but it was too late as eye contact was established. *Fuck.*

"There is no escaping." She grasped my hand tightly and looked at me with scared eyes. Those two—the women who'd birthed us—were anything but simple. They loved glamour and high-end fashion, while we were simple girls. How we could be total opposites no one understood, but it was true, and made for some very interesting battles in our homes.

We smiled then waved while walking backward toward the locker room entrance. We might have to face them at some point, but it wouldn't be right that second. Hell, no. My buzz would not be diminished by the fuckery Mom always had up her sleeve.

"I say we head back and get dirty."

My brow rose high in question while I continued to smile at our moms across the distance. "My interest has been piqued."

"Do you hear those screams of glee?"

I nodded, and her words began to make sense. Get dirty celebrating, then come and share the wealth with them. Perfect.

"HOLY SHIT!" COURTNEY YELLED THE MINUTE WE STEPPED INTO THE locker room. The chaos we had walked in on was scary in the best of ways. The semi-naked bodies of my teammates were spread about every inch of the room. Everyone was there, except for Coach Miller —and any other member of the staff with a penis, of course.

They were dancing, jumping around, and grinding against each other while they celebrated what we'd worked so hard for. Months of practice and drills that had left us in physical pain the next day. Not to mention quite the collection of bruises and scrapes from intense camps and learning new plays.

It had all culminated to this: The University of Miami's Women's Basketball Team were state champions. God, it felt good to say that.

The entire room was filled to capacity. A weird mixture of Gatorade and champagne dripped off every surface in the room. *Who managed to get this in here?* It would be our asses if we were caught.

I could only begin to imagine the faces of the janitorial staff later tonight. We'd be cursed to hell, that's for sure. Good thing the couple who did most of the cleaning after our home games were fans.

A bottle of Moet was passed to me, already half gone while I stood in the threshold, taking it all in. Helping myself to a big pull of the bubbly, I walked through the doorway and into the craziness before me.

Jennifer was down to her sports bra and shorts, shaking her ass off to the latest club hit and laughing at something someone said. "Get your asses in here," she called out over the music and sauntered our way. "We earned this shit!"

"Damn right we did." I laughed and passed the bottle over to Court.

"About time, girls." Stephanie, another teammate, pulled me into a hug while Courtney drank the remaining contents of the bottle.

"Fuck, I needed that." Court gave us all a lazy smile. "Especially if the firing squad's still outside."

"You too, huh?" Steph had grown up with us and knew the drill. While her mother wasn't as bad as ours were—it was still an equal-opportunity pony show.

"It's to be expected. We figured we'd let the crowd outside die down before we go see them." I shrugged and threw my hands up in time to catch an unopened bottle being tossed my way. "By the way, who snuck in the booze?"

"You wouldn't believe me if I told you," She laughed and took a sip of her own drink. "Just enjoy, and know that all has been taken care of."

Well that was vague.

"Can I just say that I don't envy you girls one bit?" Jen interjected before I could continue to badger Steph. Jennifer's mother was different, in a good way. She was as proud as our parents, but less in your face about it. The woman was reserved and quiet, blending in to the background and praising in private.

"Bite me, Jen," was my eloquent response.

"Maybe tomorrow?" Jen sassed before walking back over toward Courtney, leaving me in a fit of giggles.

"You know who I heard was back in town?" Stephanie's voice had gone soft. Low.

"No. Who?" I shook the bottle in my hand and pointed it at one of the seniors on the team. If my aim was dead on, she'd be hit in the boob with the cork.

"You seriously don't know? Well, shit." There was a guarded edge to her expression that sobered me up.

The bottle opened, and the cork flew straight for my victim. I heard her curse at me. Even felt the plastic bottle of water hit me in the arms. Nothing registered; my eyes were focused on a suddenly worried Steph.

My mouth opened, and the question sat on the tip of my tongue while she looked away from me. "Who's back—"

"We are champions!" Somebody screamed from the other side of the room, and everyone erupted in cheer. More bottles were popped and shaken—spraying us all in the sweet bubbly.

"Where are we heading to tonight?" Courtney yelled out from atop the bench she stood on, oblivious to my conversation with Steph. She was tipsy, her red hair damp and sticking to the side of her face. I could tell the alcohol was hitting her hard by her impromptu strip tease on one of the benches in the locker room.

She'd thrown her hands up to sing along with Jennifer while they dropped it low.

"No clue," Stephanie answered, still not meeting my eyes. She ignored the sudden elephant in the room.

"What about Rage?" Jennifer asked everyone, and I watched the smiles take over my teammates' faces. Guess that answered that.

"Cute guys and some liquor." Steph bumped me with her shoulder. "What the hell else could we need?" I got it. She was trying to steer me away from our previous conversation.

However, luck wasn't on her side.

"How about some answers? Why are you being all weird over bumping into someone? What's going on?" I demanded, taking a hold of her hand.

"I'll tell you tonight, I swear. Let's not ruin our day with shit that doesn't matter." Her eyes were pleading—begging me to understand and accept.

Nodding, I gave her fingers a squeeze and let go. "Fine, but tonight, you *will* tell me."

"Agreed."

TWO

Amanda

"You ready?" Courtney asked.

It'd been an hour since we entered the filled-to-capacity locker room. Slowly, everyone had begun to head home. There were only three of us left hanging around: Court, Steph, and me. Our mothers were waiting, and we'd run out of every excuse not to see them.

"Yeah." I nodded. "Let's get this over with." Turning toward Steph, I gave her a hug and promised to pick her up around nine, so we could get ready together at Jennifer's. She was leaving to meet up with her parents at a nearby Italian restaurant and was already running late.

"And then there were two…" Court looked about as excited as I felt. It didn't help that she was also a bit tipsy.

They were still where we'd left them. Standing by the lower bleachers, doing what they did best. We watched as they spoke animatedly with the other parents, charming the pants right off them.

Susana Brooks could be called a lot of things, but a non-existent parent she was not. Even decked out from head-to-toe in the university's colors of orange and green, she still stood out as the most beautiful woman in the room.

Other than my father's clear blue eyes and blond hair, I was my mother's clone. We shared what most would consider a beautiful bone structure. Those in her inner circle of friends always complimented on the shape of our faces and how symmetrical they were—a guideline they used often to measure beauty, too stuck in their ways to see past the superficial.

One thing I was grateful for was the small button nose my father thought looked like a tiny strawberry. His side of the family had not been so lucky; it's not that their noses were big per se, they just stood out more than most.

"Amanda," my mother called out, excusing herself before turning toward me. "About time, missy!" She stood arms open wide and waiting with a sour look on her face for me to reach her. It was ritualistic after every game; I'd hug her tight drenching her in my sweat.

I almost felt bad. She had no idea how much worse this time would be.

This time, though, her pitch hit a new level when she felt how disgusting I was. Her arms flapped rapidly, and her body shook with laughter.

"Why me, Lord?" she cried out and tried to push me away. "Just once, I'd like—"

"What were you going to say?" I'd shut her up, proudly and obnoxiously landing a huge smooch on her cheek. It was justified that I celebrate in any way I deemed right, and her annoyance was my favorite way of doing just that.

"What the hell am I now covered in young lady?" Her tone was high. It hurt my ears.

"Chill, Mom. It's just Gatorade and some alcohol we toasted with in the back." Her brow rose. "Okay, there's also my sweat, but in my defense, I am your daughter, and that should never disgust you."

"Says who?"

"Me." My muscles started to scream in protest. It'd been a while since the game ended, and my body had begun to cool off. The tension in my neck was made more pronounced by the tight bun my hair was in. Once I pulled out the pins, I couldn't stop the loud sigh of relief that escaped my lips while my blonde hair tumbled down over my shoulders.

"You should feel honored to have such an amazing athlete within the family." My mother couldn't hide her smile even if she wanted to. Annoyed or not, she was damn proud. "Can you imagine the day when I finally make it to the Olympics?"

She was eating this shit up.

"Keep talking, oh great one." Susana Brooks was known to brag about anything and everything within her reach.

"You can boast and tell all the high-society, snippety fogies you choose to surround yourself with that your daughter is the bomb."

My mother couldn't stop the laugh from escaping even if she wanted to. "What will I do with you, Mandi?" The sternness in her tone didn't fool me for even a second.

"Accept and embrace my sexy, tomboyish ways?" I asked with an all-too-sweet and innocent tone—eyes wide and searching for acceptance. My mother wasn't buying the act one bit and smacked my arm. In return, I stuck my tongue out at her.

Most that saw our relationship didn't understand it. We were different but loved one another fiercely. I'd grown up in a home where honesty was always expected. No matter the problem or how disappointed they might be, it hurt my parents the most if I lied.

"Couldn't you be a feminine and delicate athlete, instead?" She pulled my drenched body toward her. "You're a beauty, Mandi."

"I know, Mother." The woman never gave it a rest.

"Why not enhance what I gave you with some cute lowlights to accentuate those beautiful baby blues?"

I looked over at the familiar set of figures who'd joined our conversation. Thank God my best friend was coming to my rescue.

"Mandi, it could be fun," Courtney added, and then gave my mother a nod.

My smile vanished, and panic set in. "Are you high?" It was the only possible explanation for her siding with my mother.

"Think about it." She giggled. "Some lowlights wouldn't look too bad." My brow rose quizzically. "Don't look at me like that. They have organic, non-animal tested products on the market these days. At least that's what she…" her fingers pointed toward my mother's co-conspirator, her mother Kimberly, "…used in her argument."

This had set-up written all over it.

Once upon a time, when I was in love, I'd been into all the girly rituals passed on from mother to daughter. Up to a certain point, I still was, just not with the same excitement as before. When I'd thought my future had been written in the stars, before my heart had been broken, it had been easier to be carefree.

Pulling her aside, I walked us over a few feet, out of the earshot of the nosy duo. "Are you sure about this? You know how they get. We give an inch, and they take an arm."

"How bad could it be?" Court replied with a shrug like this wasn't cause for fright.

Before I could stop, my hand rose and connected with the front of her forehead in the universal *Are You Stupid* sign.

What the hell was she thinking?

"Ouch!"

"Are you insane?"

She glared at me while rubbing her forehead. "It's not that big of a deal."

"My dear friend, this could be cataclysmic and detrimental to the fight against what a woman should be in our society, and what we are. I refuse to be a Barbie. A woman with no voice expected to nod and curtsy as if this was still the golden era of kings and queens."

"A little dramatic, aren't we?" Courtney had the audacity to laugh. "You used to like doing these things if memory serves me correct, Mandi. Just because Hun—"

I had to stop her right there. He was irrelevant in my world.

"Not when you are the prodigy of one Susana Brooks, it's not. She will hold this over my head." I fisted my blonde locks and pulled. “Dammit. Knowing how conniving she is, she’ll try to mold me into a mini version of her. If I give her the tip of my pinky, she will amputate my arm and begin her quest of turning me into what she has always dreamed for me …” I trailed off as images of gowns, makeup, high heels, and snobby society gatherings began to run rampant through my mind.

“What if we compromise with them?” The cheery tone she had made me want to choke her.

“There is no compromising with them!”

“We could always just set a limit. Add a power of veto and an annulment clause to our verbal contract, in case what you foresee does become apparent in their plans.” Her smile was huge; she had me and knew it. My glare didn’t intimidate her one iota either. Instead, she rolled her eyes at me.

“That could work, Court, but screw the verbal. I want this all in writing with a third party as our witness.”

“You two are being ridiculous,” Kimberly interrupted before busting out in laughter. She’d snuck up on us, right behind Courtney who squealed like a pig in surprise.

The can of Coke Courtney was holding flew out of her hands and down the court. “Jesus, Mom, do I need to put a bell around your neck?” she hissed, hand over her chest as she tried to regulate her breathing.

“Overdramatic much, sweetheart?” her mom asked, fighting back a laugh.

“What part of private negotiations didn’t you quite understand?” my friend quipped while pointing between herself and me.

“What’s there to negotiate? We are gifting you two brats a day of beauty and relaxation.” Mock anger tinged her tone. “Instead of appreciating your gift, you’re over here preparing for battle. This is not World War Three, nor is there a need for mention of a signed contract.”

“Do you really want me to respond to that?” My brow rose. I dared her to challenge me on this. They’d done it in the past.

"Amanda!"

"Yes, Mother?"

"Oh, you." Theatrical as ever, she threw her hands up in the air then complained about her failure. In her eyes, my tomboyish tendencies were all due to my father's influence on me. All the times she'd allowed me to hang with him in our home's garage had corrupted my fragile mind. Or it could have been on the basketball court he'd put up just for me.

She never mentioned the changes my broken heart caused, and for that, I was thankful.

Courtney leaned over and whispered low enough so only I heard. "You guys are like two peas in a pod, you know?"

My mature reply was to discretely flip her off when our parent's weren't looking.

"Can we agree to an early dinner and hash out the details then?" Kimberly smiled at us. She looked like the cat who ate the canary. Too much fake innocence.

Courtney watched her every move like a hawk. She answered through narrowed eyes and pursed lips. "I don't know, Mother. *Can we*?"

"I assure you," Kimberly began, pointing toward my still ranting mother and herself, "we have nothing but honest and good intentions here. No underhanded agendas. At the end of the hour, if you two don't agree, we will not guilt or pester."

"What do you think, bestie?" I whispered. "Can we trust them?"

"I kind of think so."

"That doesn't sound too reassuring," I pointed out.

"In my defense, when mom brought it up it sounded like a good idea. No reason to be worried." Court still hadn't taken her eyes off her mother. "If at any moment we feel like this is an intervention—we leave."

"On one condition." I turned toward the too-eager-for-words matriarchs of our families.

"Of course," my mother eagerly complied. "Anything."

"You ask, and we shall deliver." Her accomplice interjected.

"Perfect." I smiled, while my best friend chuckled low. "Then you will have no problem with going in separate cars—that we drive ourselves to the restaurant after we clean up." And sober up a bit, too.

"That's not necessary—"

"Take it or leave it," I challenged Mom.

"Fine. Just hurry up and meet us outside in twenty."

THREE
Amanda

After the stare down in the gym—where neither party wanted to give an inch—our mothers relented and graciously allowed us to drive ourselves to the execution.

It wasn't that I didn't appreciate what a fabulous pair of jeans could do for one's ass; on the contrary. Feeling sexy and confident was as important to me as it was to the next woman; I just wanted to live at my own pace, set my own guidelines, and not accept what the world deemed as beautiful to dictate the way I saw myself.

If and when I felt the need to pamper myself, I did. I loved getting massages and my hair styled when needed, but I lived most of my days in between classes and practice. What use did I have for my hair to be straightened, when within the hour it would begin to curl?

"So, what's the strategy here?" Courtney fidgeted beside me. *Funny*. Back there she had been all for the non-animal-tested products and pampering. Was it finally settling in that we were fucked?

"You're an idiot," I muttered while studying the women in the car ahead of us, noticing how one laughed at something the driver said. My mother's eyes snapped to the side mirror then and locked with mine. She smiled, and I shook my head at my best friend. “What were you thinking?”

Courtney huffed beside me and ran a hand through her red hair. “She made it seem innocent! I was tricked.”

Nodding, I put on my turn signal then waited for my opening. “We can’t go in there smiling or laughing. This is war. Them against us.”

“Agreed.”

“We concede to a trim. Maybe some small color changes, but nothing too dramatic or high maintenance. I will also agree to a massage because dammit, I could use one.”

“What about pedicures or facials?” she asked.

“I got a pedi three days ago, so no. Facials are up in the air. I guess you could say it depends.”

She nodded and arched her back, stretching out her tired muscles. “Okay. I’ll give in to a pedicure and cut. I want something dramatic, though. Maybe lose the length and cut it to just below my ears.”

“With bangs?”

“That could be cute. I’ve always wanted bangs.”

Smiling, I looked over at her. “This might also be my chance to get some side swept ones.”

Courtney knew I’d always wanted them. It was something we’d discussed in the past, but like any dutiful girlfriend, I’d asked my other half for his opinion. He’d shot me down repeatedly, claiming they wouldn’t look right on me, and stupidly, I’d listened and bit my tongue.

The more time I spent apart from him, the more I realized how uneven our relationship had been. How much could someone give until they lost themselves?

Courtney laughed, bringing me back to the present. “You know, if they heard us right now they would be squealing in triumphant glory.”

“Scary. It’s definitely something they don’t need to know.” We could be girly, but at our discretion. It was our choice. *My* choice. "So, are we set?"

"Yup."

"We must stay strong, Court. No matter how thick they lay the guilt trip on us." *I hope…*

The rest of the car ride was silent as we followed them through the streets of Miami.

It seemed that my mother knew how to play dirty after all, and in this instance, my eclectic taste buds would be my downfall. I'd always been fascinated with the Brazilian culture, and Fogo de Chao was the best churrascaria we had in town.

"She didn't."

"Oh, fuck, Mandi. That's—"

"I know." My gulp inside the car was loud while we pulled up to the valet parking. "They played us dirty. Used our stomachs against us."

"It'll be okay. We know them; this isn't something we can't ignore." Her stomach rumbled then—as loud as my gulp. Can't ignore, my ass.

Three summers ago, our families had traveled to Rio de Janeiro Brazil, and had fallen in love. I'd been lucky enough to see, with my own eyes, the wonderment that the country held. We'd experienced it all, from the world's best beaches to their food. The Tijuca National Park was fun to explore, and it was something my father and I did together. The Lapa neighborhood, with its famous steps and bars, had made us feel alive. Music everywhere—people dancing—celebrating love and life. However, it had been the Christ the Redeemer statue that stole my breath away. Majestic and otherworldly, it stood proud overlooking the city. Its beauty couldn't be measured.

Simply put, it had been the best family vacation ever, and now, it was biting me in the ass.

The restaurant opened a year after we returned, quickly becoming a local stomping ground for the Brooks' family. So much so, the staff now knew to expect us at least twice a week for dinner.

"Not a scratch," I told the drooling, pimpled-faced attendant when he openly gaped at my '69 mustang. This car was my pride and joy. A special project I'd taken on with my father, it took us a year to complete, but it was worth every scrape and bruise I sustained. It was a beauty: cherry red and all shiny chrome—the envy of every mid-life crisis fool in the city of Miami.

Growing up, dad wasn't around much. Not because he didn't want to be, but being a member of the city's council is a twenty-four hour job here. I understood that. The man was hard-working and loved us fiercely; any time he was able to give was appreciated.

"Yes, ma'am," the kid replied while I put the keys to my baby in his waiting palm. His hands shook as he opened the door and got in, his face too jubilant for my liking.

Fucker didn't know how to handle so much power.

"Leave the poor kid alone, Amanda." My mother appeared next to me, smiling at our conversation. "Maybe, if he crashes it, I could buy you one of those cute little Fiats to replace it." She was full of shit.

My mother loved the car as much as I did; she had enjoyed every second Dad and I worked on it. Dirty, greased-up smudges and kisses had made her smile while we brought that beauty to life.

"You wouldn't," I gasped out in mock horror. "Then again, maybe Dad and I could rebuild something new for me?"

Kimberly laughed at my mother's horrified face. "Didn't see that one coming, Susana?"

She ignored Kimberly's jab and grabbed my hand. "Come on, my darling brat. We have much to discuss and plan."

"Jesus," Courtney mumbled.

Kimberly shook her head and pushed her daughter toward the door. "You two are being ridiculous."

"Funny, Mom," Court deadpanned. "Have you and Aunt Susana looked in the mirror lately?"

I laughed. What else could I do but laugh at the craziness that was my life?

"Can we go in already?" Mom whined.

"Bite me, Susana." Kimberly rolled her eyes.

"And you two are the adults?" Court sighed and turned to face me. "We are so screwed." Sadly, I could only nod in acceptance of what would be us one day.

"Oh hush, you two, and walk in." Kim sneered, while my mother muttered something about *kids and smart mouths.*

As usual, the place smelled amazing when we entered. The scent of grilling meat made us all moan quietly. I know. Disturbing.

"Evening, Mrs. Brooks," Fernanda, the hostess, greeted. "Will it be just the four of you today?"

"Yes, dear," Mom replied. "By the way, is Carlos working tonight?"

"Yes, ma'am."

"Then we would like a table in his section if it isn't too much trouble."

"Of course," Fernanda said with a smile. "Right this way."

Once seated—the mothers on one side with Court and me on the other—the pythons began to guilt us. In reality, I was surprised my mother had stayed quiet for so long.

"Baby girl, the day you were born," she gushed, "was the happiest day of my life. I'd always dreamed of having a little girl, and there you were. I wanted to dress you up, play Barbie's, and as you got older, take care of your heart when some jerk broke it. Everything your grandmother wasn't able to do with me before her passing." *Oh, that's a low blow, Mom.* "So beautiful and tiny in my arms. All ten toes and fingers accounted for. You had your father's eyes and hair, while your lips and nose were mine. What I held was perfection."

Dammit, cue my tears and hers.

"I want us to do this together, Amanda. We should bond like you and Daddy do over cars. Think of it this way: instead of getting dirty and grimy, I want to pamper you. Go to the spa and get our nails done. Maybe a massage? Talk about boys?"

Kim reached across the table, grabbed both our hands, and squeezed. "You girls are in college now; you've grown up right before our eyes into amazing women. All we want is to spend some quality time with you before you find your own prince charming and leave us."

The tears started flowing. They'd won.

"I love you, Mom," Courtney and I whispered together.

"We know, babies, and we love you, too. All we ask is that you consider this; think it through before turning us down. I—*we* don't want to change you. You both couldn't be any more perfect in our eyes."

"Okay," I spoke through the lump forming in my throat.

"Okay?" Kim repeated in question.

"Yeah, let's do this thing. But—" Court began only to be interrupted by her mom.

"Why is there always a 'but'?"

"Because I have stipulations," Courtney replied, her fingers still wiping the falling tears from her cheeks.

"We," I added in a no-nonsense tone, "will consent." They smiled wide and wiggled a bit in their seats. "However…" I pointed toward them "…we have the right to veto if you take it too far." The matriarchs nodded, albeit with some reluctance. "No drastic changes of any kind."

Kimberly opened her mouth to refute, but Court knew her too well and steamrolled right over her attempts. "At the end of the day, we want to look like ourselves, not you. Agree, and we will attend the monthly dates."

"Three," Mom countered.

"One." I stood strong.

"Two?" Kim tried.

"Fine." The entire negotiation scene between us made the older woman, the next table over, laugh.

"We agree to your terms, but—" *That 'but' scares me, Mom.*

"The first mother-daughter date will be in four days. A full day where we will be pampered from head-to-toe."

"You already had this planned, didn't you?" Of course, she had. I looked over at my best friend and she looked just as dumbfounded as I felt. We'd fallen for the mother/daughter love of my life bullshit again.

There was never a doubt on how much they loved us, but Jesus. We fell for it completely.

"Of course," Mom said with a giggle. "And the guy I found for you is perfect. Camden Daniels is known for working with athletes, and from what I heard, he has magical hands. You will thank me after." The mischief behind her eyes should have alerted me to how screwed I would be.

What had I just agreed to?

FOUR

Amanda

"You're late." Jennifer greeted us with a tray of Jell-O shots in her hand, the multi-flavored little offerings making my mouth water.

"Blame that one." I pointed at Steph, and then took one of the tiny cups with the delicious concoction inside. It tasted so good. The liquor slid down my throat and I moaned out a low, *fuck*.

"Been a while, Mandi?

"Be specific, dork."

Flipping me off, she threw back her own shot. "Since, you know…you've been fucked properly?"

I rolled my eyes at her. "Way too long." They all knew it had been. It'd taken me two years to find myself after he left. Hunter was all I knew.

Together since middle school, I'd loved him fiercely but that hadn't been enough for him. He'd wanted to taste what the world had to offer, and that hurt more than anything. His words had made me feel small, like I wasn't enough.

I was ready to feel that kind of connection again. Not a relationship with all the feelings attached, no. What I yearned for was a man's touch. To be taken. Fucked. Worshipped.

"Amen." We all turned to look at Courtney. "What? It's true," she laughed.

"Well…" *This was new.* Jennifer blushed and looked away.

"Spill, bitch." Grabbing her by the arm, I dragged her in to the living room and placed the tray of shots on her coffee table. "Did you get laid?"

"When?" Steph demanded as we surrounded a giggling Jennifer. "And for the love of God, woman, with who?"

Jennifer covered her face with her hand and her muffled response left us speechless. "I slept with Coach Miller yesterday."

Holy…

"Shit!" Courtney laughed, and the rest of us followed. The man was young for the position he held. Only thirty-six and single, he had every woman on our team drooling, and that heifer had slept with him.

"Well, cheers to that." Everyone followed my lead and threw a shot back. "Congrats, babe."

"Can I just say that I'm proud to call you a friend?" Stephanie stood up and bowed before Jen. "Now, how big is he?"

"Damn. You beat me to it." Court reached for the tray and grabbed another shot. "Was he impressive? We've seen his hands and feet. Is he as big as we all want him to be?"

"Those long fingers." I fanned myself and joined Courtney in having another shot.

"I cannot believe I'm admitting this." Jennifer stood up, walked over, and opened the side table by the couch. She pulled a measuring tape from within and measured out nine inches. "Very thick, too."

"You lucky bitch." It was the only way I could express how I felt. Impressive would be an understatement. "How the hell did you play today? You should be sore."

"Trust me, I am." Her face said it all. She looked smug, and in my opinion, she had every right to be.

"Nice." Stephanie's face was comical. She wore an expression mixed between jealousy and pride. "Now, let's hurry up and get ready. I'm hoping to get lucky and meet someone tonight."

"One-night stands aren't your norm," Jennifer said what I was thinking.

"Yes, and that isn't the case for tonight either." Steph grabbed her bag from the floor and stood up. She eyed the last shot on the table before grabbing it and tossing it back. "I'm hoping to meet someone, not fuck them. The cock riding comes much later in the relationship."

"Amen," I agreed, and followed her toward the guest bedroom.

Jennifer's parents paid for this amazing apartment off Brickell Ave. It was a spacious, two-bedroom condominium close to both the bay and the nightlife downtown Miami offered.

The other two split off and began to get dressed in Jennifer's room. Steph and I took the guest room and bathroom as ours.

"What time are the others meeting us, Mandi?" Stephanie rummaged through her bag and pulled out a little black number. It was a simple, sweetheart-neckline dress that was tight on the body and ended mid-thigh. She pulled her hair into a sleek bun at the nape of her neck. For shoes, she had a pair of black pumps, and then some gold teardrop earrings to finalize her look. She looked beautiful.

I whistled in approval. "Cute dress."

"Thanks."

"By the way, we agreed at ten in front of Rage."

Steph looked down at her watch and snapped her fingers at me. "Fuck, Mandi, it's nine already. Finish up, while I go and hurry the others."

Waving her off, I shimmied into my pair of distressed skinny jeans. They were tight, and molded onto my curves perfectly. Eyeing the two tops I'd brought, I turned to the mirror and pulled them in front of me.

Did I want attention?

To show off the curves hours at the gym had given me?

Or did I want to go with comfortable?

"Do it."

I looked up then and caught Courtney's eye in the mirror. "What?"

"You're thinking about him again, aren't you?"

"It's not—"

"Fuck him and show some skin. Flaunt what you worked your ass off for."

She was right. It'd been so long since he left—he'd abandoned our relationship the moment he was accepted into NYU. The twinge of hurt still simmered, but I was at the stage where breathing didn't cripple me. I no longer loved him, just missed what we had.

The flimsy, light pink, crocheted halter-top felt light in my hands while I pulled it into position. "Can you tie me up?"

"The men tonight will be falling over themselves when they see you. Prepare to be eye-fucked all night." Court tied the top securely with a small smile on her face. "It's nice to see you be yourself again."

"I've always been here."

"In a physical sense, yes. Sometimes, though, you'd be right in front of me, but mentally miles away." Courtney placed her hands on my shoulders and gave them a squeeze. "Love's a bitch, I get that, Mandi. That's why I never pushed."

"Thank you." I squeezed her hand on my shoulder and finished getting ready.

A few gold bangles and some hoop earrings worked well with the outfit. Fingering the long gold necklace he'd bought me the last birthday we were together, I was tempted to put it on.

No. Courtney was right. *Fuck him.*

I kept the makeup light, just some liner and tinted gloss to polish my look. What stared back at me from the mirror made me smile. It was me. The *me* from before he'd left.

The girls were all sitting in the living room when I walked out. Jennifer and Courtney were keeping it simple tonight with similar bandage dresses. Jen's dress was red—bright and sexy. It matched her strong personality. Her long, dark hair was up in a high ponytail and her makeup was simple except for the bold red lips which matched her dress.

Courtney's dress was silver and short. Her long red hair had been kept down, the natural waves framing her face softly. Like me, she'd kept her face clean and only wore gloss.

"Ready to go?" I asked while slipping my wedged sandals on. The girls were in similar positions, bent over and securing their strappy heels in place.

"Hell yes!" they yelled out in unison and then laughed. There was a bottle of tequila on the center table that hadn't been there before.

It was time to call a cab. There was no way in hell any of us would be sober enough to drive back.

We were late.

More than forty minutes behind schedule, in fact, so we'd called the other girls to wait for us. The nighttime traffic tonight was ridiculous. Everyone in the city was out celebrating and drinking to one thing or another, most, like us, taking taxis to their destinations.

"Jesus." Steph whistled at the line before us. It wrapped around the building, toward the small parking area at the rear.

"Who's working the door?" Reaching into my back pocket, I pulled out a few bills and paid the cabbie. We'd asked the driver to leave us a block away. Any closer, and we'd be lucky to get there by morning.

Courtney giggled while pulling her dress down. "I think Kevin is, Mandi."

"Shit," I grouched and turned to wave the taxi back. Kevin has had a crush on me for the last year. He'd asked me out countless times. I simply wasn't interested.

"He's cute," Steph argued, and I raised a brow. "Amanda, he's—"

"Not my type." My tone had come out harsher than intended, but they needed to back off. It wasn't the first time they'd tried to sell someone of the opposite sex to me.

"Guys, leave Mandi alone."

I gave Jennifer a grateful smile and accepted her outstretched hand. "Thank you."

"No problem, babe."

We walked off toward the club. The other two reached us soon enough, apologetic puppy dog eyes in place. "Sorry." They said in unison, and I nodded in acceptance. They meant well; it wasn't their fault that I'd yet to meet a man who'd steal my breath.

Who'd take me to the edge and let me fall, wrapped up in his arms.

There were many glares and curses when we bypassed the line and went straight for the club's main doors. Kevin was off tonight, and I sighed in relief, much to the other bouncer's amusement.

"The VIP section has been reserved for you girls tonight. Your party is already upstairs enjoying."

"We didn't request—"

He cut me off, smirk in place, while looking down at his clipboard. "A Susana Brooks requested it for you and she left her credit card on file to cover the tab."

"Holy shit!" That came from me.

"Love your mom, Mandi." Steph clapped twice and walked past me. The other two followed while I watched at a loss.

I couldn't believe she'd done this. *How did she even know we were coming here?*

"I told Mom we'd be here tonight," Court answered my unvoiced question. "Pretty cool of her." And she was right. This was beyond nice of her.

My phone pinged then. I pulled it from my back pocket and

opened the screen to my messages. Mom had sent me a text fifteen minutes ago. Only one word: *Enjoy.*

The walls inside the club thumped. It was reggae night and the space was packed to capacity, bodies grinding and more ass on display than any strip club in town. The décor inside of Rage was a mixture of industrial chic meets brothel. Clean lines and sex. Steel-paneled walls and long leather couches. Smooth concrete floors and vintage chandeliers. It was an odd mix, yet it worked.

"What are you drinking?" Jennifer yelled over the music as we walked toward the VIP sections. "I'm in a vodka kind of mood."

"With OJ?" It was the only way, in my book, to drink vodka.

"Is there any other way?"

"I want mine with cranberry instead," Court added, while shaking her head at some overdone pretty boy who tried to pull her away to dance.

Jennifer nodded and pulled a silent Steph along with her to the private bar close by. We found our section and sat down. It seemed the rest of our team was already out on the floor.

"Have you heard from Hunter yet?" Court's question caught me off guard. We didn't mention him often, let alone say his name, the conversation we had in Jennifer's bedroom being a rarity.

"No." He was the last person I wanted to see. I was over his lies and my mother's desire to see me back with him.

How did one walk away from the person they claimed to love because they wanted to explore? What kind of heartless person just went off to college to sample the buffet without feeling the guilt afterward?

Hunter broke my heart simply because he wanted to be able to fuck around guilt-free, without our relationship stopping him.

"Do you want to hear from him?"

What the fuck was she getting at? "Again, no. Why are we even talking about him?"

She sighed and looked past my shoulder and toward the bar. "I heard he was back."

My chest constricted. Fuck, did it hurt. "What? When?"

"Don't know, just heard he was around, and asking." Her eyes snapped back to mine, and the sadness there made my own water. "Just don't want to see you lose yourself, Mandi. When he left, it was like you left too."

Rubbing a hand over my face, I took in a deep breath. It didn't help. The sting was still there, but it had gone from painful to anger. "I don't love him anymore, if that's what you're worried about."

She tilted her head to the side and studied me. "That's good to know, but—"

"No 'but'. He lost me the moment he threw us away."

Courtney seemed satisfied by my answer and let the conversation drop as the others neared. Steph passed her a drink, and the two shared a look.

"Wait a minute," I hissed out, and slammed my hand on the table. "Is that what…fuck! Did you see Hunter?"

Steph took a huge gulp of her drink and nodded. "He came to practice while you were out with the flu."

That son of a bitch. What the hell did he think coming to see me would solve? It's been two years, dammit.

"Fuck him, Mandi." Jennifer pushed a drink into my hand and urged me to take a sip. I did, and the cold, citrusy liquid felt good going down. Smooth. It warmed me a bit and I began to relax.

"You're right. Fuck him. Hunter Knox will not ruin my night." The girls applauded and pulled me out to the dance floor. I let the island rhythms take me away from thoughts of him. My body moved to the beat, a slow sensual roll of my hips that caught the eyes of a few men on the floor.

A few women, too.

Not interested.

Closing my eyes, I dreamed of finding the right man. How he'd hold me close as we danced, his body dwarfing mine, making me feel small and delicate. Safe.

He would be tall…

"One so beautiful should never wear such a sad expression." The whispered words against my neck made me gasp, and the arms of the stranger wrapped around me, pulled me tight against his chest.

A hard chest. Defined. All man.

"What—" I began and tried to turn in his arms. Those arms tightened around me, halting my movement.

"Shhh, beautiful. Let me hold you." It was a rough plea.

Nodding, I complied and started to move against him. My insides fluttered as he skimmed his lips along my throat. Goosebumps rose all over my skin when he kissed me, twice, below my ear. It was erotic—gratifying to feel wanted.

"I'd like to see you." The neediness in my tone caught me off guard. *What's happening to me*?

"I've had my eyes on you all night." He groaned, pushing his hardened cock against my ass. I should have been appalled. Pissed off at his actions.

It had the opposite effect.

"Then why did it take you so long to approach?" Swiveling my hips, I dropped down low, and worked my way up his body. With each gyration against him, he pushed harder, using my fleshy rear to create the friction he needed.

Hard. Thick. Big.

"Just biding my time. There was no doubt in my mind that I'd have you by the end of the night." *Cocky son of a bitch.*

Before he could stop me, I turned around. My eyes met his, and then…it went dark. Pitch-black dark inside the club. People complained while I stood still.

His eyes had been wild like the sea and just as beautiful. They were all I was able to focus on for the two seconds I had him in front of me.

The light flickered twice, and I reached out for him. He grabbed my hand and tugged—I felt the warmth of his skin covering mine. Like a wild inferno that raged within my veins, it burned to have him this close.

“I’ll see you again,” my stranger whispered before his lips met mine in a gentle kiss. It was the complete opposite of every moment we’d shared on the dance floor.

“How? What’s your name?”

“Trust me.” He nipped my bottom lip once more, and then he was gone. I was left in the middle of the dance floor horny and confused.

The lights came back on then. Everyone around me continued with their night of fun while I suffered the loss of him. All I had of my sexy stranger were his smoldering eyes, and it wasn’t enough.

I needed more to satisfy the sudden thirst he’d created.

FIVE
Amanda

"Amanda Kailey Brooks, for God's sake, child," my mother yelled from the bottom of the stairs. "Get down here. You're going to make us late."

It had been four days since I agreed to her daughter/mother day, and she was already pushing my buttons. Didn't help that it had also been four days of extreme sexual frustration. A frustration so consuming that I felt lost.

Four days since the club, and I couldn't get him, or his haunting eyes, out of my mind. So much so, that I'd woken up twice since that night with my hand down my panties and those enslaving eyes pushing me toward my euphoric descent.

No one, not even Hunter, had sparked this much desire from me. And all we'd done was dance.

"Hurry up," she called again, exasperated.

"Dear God," I whimpered while my eyes adjusted, and I looked over at my alarm clock. It was barely nine in the morning. *Why me?* Taking in a deep breath, I swung my legs over the bed then stumbled across my room and into the closet.

"I'm coming!"

"If we miss our appointments…" she began.

"Keep it up, and I'll go back to bed. Pain in the butt old lady." The last part I muttered under my breath. Stupid, I was not.

"Do it, and I'll pour a bucket of freezing water on your head while you snore."

"Keep pushing, and I'll wear the rattiest sweats and tank I own."

"You wouldn't dare," she huffed. I heard the creak of the stairs as she made her way up.

"You know I would."

"Mandi, please." She stood outside my door now, dressed in a simple coral dress and tan-colored sandals. "We need to leave in an hour, and your breakfast is getting cold—"

"Why didn't you start by mentioning the food first? I'm starved."

Mom laughed and joined me in the closet. "You're always hungry." She reached out and pulled a short, white sundress for me to wear. I'd forgotten about that one. It was soft and comfortable. Perfect.

"Which shoes? The gold pair that wrap up my calves or the plain white flats?"

"Definitely the gold pair." Mom grabbed the shoes in question and pushed them into my hands. "Now hurry up, I made pancakes."

"Yes, drill sergeant!" Her eyes narrowed as she came closer. I had no chance to defend myself. She attacked me with the towel that lay over the overstuffed chair inside my walk-in. "Quit it!"

"Promise me you'll be ready in thirty minutes and I will."

"Cross my heart." I giggled and dodged her next hit. "Where did you learn to use that as a weapon?"

"Your father and I—"

"Stop right there." Gagging, I pulled the towel away. "That's more than I need to know, plus I need to get ready. So, out."

"And they say I'm the overdramatic one." With that, she gave me a kiss and walked out. The entire exchange had left me with fifteen minutes to shower and eat.

Happy pampering day to me.

"ABOUT TIME."

Ignoring my mother's jab, I walked over to the table and sat down. My plate was already stacked with pancakes; the butter and syrup placed in the center of the table.

The noises my stomach made caused me to blush.

Mom laughed then set a glass of juice beside my plate. "Eat."

"Do we have time?" I asked drowning the flapjacks in syrup.

"Yes." She sighed. "I called and pushed our appointments back. We have an extra hour."

Good. In all honesty, I wasn't in any hurry to get up and spend my day with the pretentious women that resided here. The Coco Plum area in Coral Gables was known for its opulence and ridiculously rich families in Miami.

It was an area where every house was bigger than the last, and how much money you had was all that mattered. Not everyone was like that though—no, not everyone.

My best friend Courtney Ellis and her family were one of those rare gems. Courtney never relied on her beauty to get ahead in life. Sure, she was aware of the effect she had on the opposite sex with her bright red hair, wide green eyes, and tight athletic body. She stood for something, though; she was more than just another pretty face in the crowd. Her measure in life didn't come from what her father bought her or the kind of car she drove.

"Love you, Mom."

"Brat." She huffed, trying to look put out but it didn't work. A smirk graced her lips when I stuck my tongue out at her.

Looking over at the juice, I eyed it with disdain. "Can I have coffee instead?" Shoving another forkful in, I chewed and swallowed before speaking. "Please."

"Too much caffeine is bad for you."

Bullshit. She drank more coffee and soda than anyone I knew. "But—"

Mom rolled her eyes and held her hand up. "Drink that, and I'll get you something caffeinated to go."

I didn't want *something*, I wanted coffee.

However, instead of complaining and annoying her any further, I simply ate and enjoyed my food. "So." I took a sip of the juice and grimaced. The bitterness of grapefruit never sat well with me. It tasted horrible. "What's on the agenda today? What should I be prepared for?"

"I want you to get a trim with some possible low-lights framing your face. Then, I want you to be worked out—a deep-tissue massage should do the trick. I'm sure you will find perfection there."

"Anything else?" I asked, pointing my fork at her.

"Nope."

That reply came too fast. It didn't help settle my nerves. "By the way, you keep mentioning that I'll love who you picked. Should I be concerned? Does Dad know about this masseur fetish/fascination you seem to have?"

Mom rolled her eyes, but the smile never vanished. "Absolutely not. Just thought you might find what you've been missing." That was vague. "Enjoy the eye candy, Mandi. Just not too much, he's…"

"He's what?"

"Too old for you."

Well, there went my visions of someone hot with magical hands. The last thing I wanted was some old pervert feeling me up. After that declaration, I went back to eating a lot slower than before. By that point, I was annoyed and didn't want to go. *Why couldn't she just let me be?*

I would never be like her, but she would never stop dreaming.

Mom had fantasies of things that would never be. Of a wedding with the perfect candidate in her eyes—with me dressed in white, and being walked down the aisle to the man she wished for me.

"Good morning, girls." Dad snorted when he entered the kitchen with two white paper bags in hand. He'd been to the Cuban bakery down the street already, thank God. "What are the plans for today?" *As if he didn't know.*

Mom laughed and sidled up next to him, her hands going around his waist while she hugged him tight. "Just spending the day together. You know, girl time."

"Can it, you two," I hissed and grabbed my bag. "I'm being sent off for torture, and you two find this amusing?"

Dad raised a brow and turned to look at Mom. "She got the dramatic flair from you, dear."

"I've never denied it, love." Mom squeezed him tight once more, then pulled away and walked toward the counter where a to-go cup sat. With her back turned to us, she poured some hot liquid in and placed the lid on top. "Ready?"

"What's this?"

"Your something caffeinated," she stated, giddiness coloring her tone. Dad tried to hide his chuckle as I took a sip of the piping hot liquid.

What the fuck?

"No." I was ready to commit murder as she pushed me toward the front door. Why would she think that green tea would ever be a good substitute for coffee? What had I ever done to warrant such cruelty?

"Stop pouting," she said while giggling. "It's good for you."

"Then you drink it, and hand over the *colada* Dad brought you."

"Now, Mandi," Dad began, "be nice to your mother. She's only trying to do something nice for you."

"Dad, you know I love you, right?"

"What's it going to cost me?" He shook his head with arms crossed over his chest and stared me down.

"Oh, my God! I only did that once, and you refuse to let it go. You're worse than Mom." They gasped, and then burst into a laughing fit. My parents were the shit.

Going to school so close to home afforded me the luxury of living at home. I still had the pleasure of morning banters and family meals. It was fun. They weren't into smothering me, so I had the freedom to come and go as I pleased.

Eyeing the cup of Cuban coffee in her hand, I took a step toward her. "If it's so good, why don't we switch?"

A war was seconds away from erupting within the Brooks' home if she didn't hand it over.

Mom shook her head while taking a sip. "Nope."

I glared and reached out for the Styrofoam cup. "Give it."

"Have fun, girls. I'm off to the office," Dad interrupted and kissed both our cheeks. "I trust you both to be on your best behavior. I don't want to receive phone calls today complaining about bratty mothers or stubborn daughters. Understood?"

"Yes, sir." We both mock saluted and gave him a hug. The man was a saint to put up with our craziness.

"Come on, missy. Time's a wasting and there's much to do." She gave me the rest of the hot concoction in her hand. The first sip tasted like heaven.

"Why do I feel like I've sold my soul to the devil?"

"Because you did." Mom looked entirely too proud of herself. It scared me more than the threat of hair color and strange hands molding my flesh ever would.

She was up to something; I just didn't know what…yet.

"YOU GET BROWNIE POINTS FOR THE LOCATION, MOM," COURTNEY declared from her seat beside me, and I agreed. The spa they'd chosen was located inside one of the trendier hotels in the city.

The Ritz Carlton had always been one of the most relaxing and opulent experiences a person would ever have. Court and I weren't ashamed one bit of being ecstatic when we arrived. The entire place had a West Indian-Caribbean vibe to it with its light colors and relaxed atmosphere.

"Glad you girls are excited. Now," Kimberly began, "we want you on your best behavior, and no bitching over what has been discussed. If either of you…" she pointed at each of us "…plans at any moment to use your power of veto, you will pull us aside and state it."

Courtney stared at them, eyes narrowed. "As long as you understand that our veto is final and not up for discussion?" My mother and her accomplice nodded. "Then we shall have no altercations or embarrassing moments today."

"Dear God," Mom cried out, "could you two be any more—"

"Watch it, lady. I'm playing your game." I raised a brow and dared her to challenge me. She huffed but didn't say a word as we pulled up to the hotel's valet parking. The attendant was about our age, maybe a few years older. He never spared us a glance, eyes fixed on my mother instead.

"Hey, buddy," I hissed at him. "She's married. Back off." He took the keys from my mother's hand and scurried off, embarrassed, and more than likely willing his small dick to calm down. No child ever wants to see her mother being checked out. Not cool by any means.

Once inside, we were handed our itineraries.

"Enjoy and behave." They didn't spare us another look, just walked past us toward the hotel's pool area. It was weird.

"So where are you heading off to?" I asked while skimming over my own appointment sheet.

"Um…" Courtney's eyes reviewed her itinerary. "She set me up with a Thai-Chi class before my appointment with someone named Simone to cut my hair. You?"

"I'm heading down to the spa for a massage from a man named Camden. She swears he's amazing." I shrugged.

"Lucky bitch. While I'm stuck taking a class, you'll be relaxing and being worked on."

"Shut it and hurry up. You have five minutes to get changed and ready for your work out." After a quick hug, we parted ways.

Checking in for my massage was quick, and I was led over to a quaint little sitting area to wait for Camden.

Seemed he was running a bit late. Great.

A plush, couch sat against the wall in the Spa's waiting area. It was comfortable, and if it weren't frowned upon, I would have easily taken a nap.

A tall, blonde woman sat behind the reception desk typing away. She ignored me as I did her. It was more than obvious that she wasn't paid to entertain the clientele as everyone else had done up to this point. She lacked basic customer service skills.

"Care for something to drink?" she asked snidely, catching me off guard. How she'd managed to get this job was beyond me.

"Sure. Anything will be fine." If my mother would've been here, she would have claimed the lady's aura stunk. It was her nice way of calling a bitch, a bitch.

So lost was I in my own musings that I failed to see him walk in. His voice had a deep cadence—made to sexually destroy and disarm those around him. A voice that was familiar.

My nipples pebbled as his scent carried into the room. It was a combination of man and the sea. A nautical concoction—the unique blend of sweat and lust riddled my brain useless. It left me frozen on their comfortable couch. Never had I reacted so strongly to a member of the opposite sex.

That's a lie. My sexy stranger had also had me at his mercy with just a few whispered words.

"Is my next appointment here, Cynthia?"

My eyes traveled up his form and ate every single detail they could, committing it all down to memory and saving it for later use. His body was lean, the muscles of his back rippled as he stretched up. A sliver of tan skin came into view, and I bit my lip to cage in the whimper that begged to erupt.

He had a swimmer's body. Perfection.

"Hi, Camden," the tramp simpered, and my fists clenched. *Shit, where did this reaction come from?* "She's sitting right there, handsome. Do you need *help* setting up? You know I'm *always* willing to lend a hand."

"Yet, have I *eve*r taken you up on the offer?" Camden seemed annoyed by her offering. Almost disgusted.

She pouted, her eyes heavy with lust. "There's always a first time."

Enough of this shit. I cleared my throat in annoyance. "I'm ready when you are."

At the sound of my voice, he turned my way and looked me up and down. If I'd thought he was spectacular from the view his profile afforded me, then he was lethal when facing me head-on.

There was no doubt in my mind. He would be more than trouble.

SIX
Amanda

"Are you, now?" He seemed amused, lip curling just a tiny bit on the left. The perfect fucking smirk on those kissable lips. "I'm Camden, by the way, and I'll be taking care of your needs."

"I have things to do today, Camden." His named flowed from my lips on a tiny moan. With reverence and desire. "There's a lot on my agenda."

All bullshit of course, but he didn't need to know that.

Closing my fists, I held them clenched in my lap. The movement caused him to lower his aquamarine eyes and bite his succulent bottom lip. I felt his stare; felt the heat of it roam over my bare legs.

Goosebumps rose on my skin when his eyes—eyes that reminded me of my sexy stranger—stared me down. My body trembled, and a small wave of pulsating need rocked through every cell of my body. It shook me to the core.

How was this possible? The same eyes…it couldn't be.

"I see." He frowned, his jaw ticking as he watched me. "Sorry for the delay, my little *gatita*. Right this way." Camden's intense stare never wavered in its perusal while I stood; on the contrary, his visual caress only intensified the closer to him I got.

My stomach muscles contracted with each breath I took. His eyes darkened, and my clit twitched. What, at first view, looked to be a calming sea of tranquility quickly morphed into a raging storm of lust.

Once within touching distance, the need to reach out to him only grew fiercer. I pulled on his arms—daring and saying a big fuck you to the inappropriate—tugging him just a bit closer. The ardor that simple contact ignited made me light-headed. The blood pulsed through my veins for him.

"I'll forgive your tardiness on one condition." The whispered words in the silence of the room felt like a war cry. Embarrassment rose on my cheeks and I grew warm under his intense scrutiny.

His finger reached out and tilted my face up. "I'm listening."

"Tell me why you call me a 'tiny kitty' in *Spanish*?" His smile was back, making him look youthful and coquettish.

"You."

What the hell kind of an answer was that? Narrowing my eyes, I asked, "Me?"

He lowered the finger holding my chin in place and wrapped his arm around my waist. It was completely inappropriate, I knew. The huff behind us from where the plastic bimbo receptionist sat told me she agreed.

"Yes, *gatita*. You are one delicate little wild pussy that I plan to set free."

I flushed red at his words. It wasn't out of anger or embarrassment. No. It was raw lust and greed for more that made me blush. "But why in Spanish?"

"Because I could easily talk about that sweet pink pussy in public and no one would be the wiser. They'd see the name as cute, when in reality, I'm letting the world know that this little kitty will only purr for me."

Oh God. My heart raced, and my palms became sweaty. Camden squeezed my side, and I trembled. No words were spoken—none were needed. The cocky son of a bitch had me. Twice in the last few days, I'd been rendered an aroused mess. Was I in such desperate need for a man's touch that any would do?

No, it couldn't be. I refused to believe that.

It was undeniable the spark I felt as his larger frame dwarfed mine. Raw masculinity oozed out of every pore of his body; it made my inner bitch want to submit my soul to his every desire.

"UNDRESS FOR ME."

Three words filled the silence of his room. The door had barely closed when he uttered them, undoing the small bit of decorum I'd tried to hold onto.

It didn't help that I felt his presence behind me. Camden stood just a mere foot away and took in deep breaths, filling his lungs with my scent. His body heat branded—engulfed me. In that moment, I wanted to burn for him.

To let him see the red hot blaze of fire that swam through my veins as his hand pushed me just a bit closer to the massage table.

"Is there somewhere…a bathroom for me to change?" Breathing labored and cheeks flushed, I continued to face forward. This man—motherfucking gorgeous male specimen—couldn't know what his mere presence did to me.

"No." This time, my head snapped back and took him in. Camden was dead serious.

"Okay," I spoke lowly, "are you going to exit the room, then?"

"No." His gruff tone caused my body to release a small tremble. I felt it down to my bones. "Now, undress for me."

Camden didn't leave. Instead, he walked backward toward the door and stood before it, leaned back, and waited for me to finish. The voice inside my head, my conscience, told me to walk out and demand someone else. My foot took a small step forward, just one measly little step, and then stopped.

"Amanda." The pure, rough sensuality in his timber made me whimper. Fuck me, I had to get out.

"I'm going to—"

"Look at me," Camden commanded, and my eyes obeyed. They snapped up and took him in. "You aren't going anywhere, nor are you getting someone else. Get that thought out of your head, now."

I shook my head, trying to clear the dirty thoughts his dominating actions created.

"Undress." This time it was my traitorous hands that followed as they tried to lower the zipper to my dress. Fingers trembling, I fumbled, lacking the concentration needed to follow directions.

Looking at his over six-foot frame made me nervous. At five foot six, I was the smallest point guard in our college division, a difference I've never really noticed when facing taller opponents. With him, I felt every inch of our difference.

"You want this—me, just like you did that night at Rage."

Fuck me, it *was* him? It was him that I responded to in this way.

"That was you?" was my weak reply. Out of all the things I could have said, I stated the obvious.

He moved closer still. Right in front of me, my face leveled with his well-defined chest. "I can see it with every inhale you take. The way your lips part and your tongue darts out to moisten them as you look at me."

"I can't…fuck."

"Turn around." He demanded, and I did. Camden's long fingers moved my hair away from my neck and set it to the side. If it was possible, he pulled himself closer. Breathed me in deep and groaned loud. "You smell of innocence and sex. How the fuck is that even possible?"

"Camden, I—" He ignored me, his sole attention on lowering the zipper of my dress.

It was slow. Torturous how he lowered the only thing keeping me covered. I turned my face and watched his reaction from over my shoulder. Once the zipper was down, he simply stood back and watched as the short, strapless white dress pooled at my feet. He admired every inch of skin that became visible.

"Turn around." Camden's voice was gruff and deep. It washed over my skin like a fiery caress. I wanted to hide myself, but those lust-filled eyes held me locked in place. The sight of him breathing hard, lip caught between his teeth, made me feel proud. I'd caught his attention.

Not the Barbie outside.

Not some other client.

Me.

Smiling up at him, I twirled a piece of my blonde hair in my finger. "Why?"

He chuckled, his hand rubbing his jaw. "Because I need to know…"

"Know what?"

"What the good Lord has blessed me with." I turned slowly at his words. On a subconscious level, my reactions to him scared me. The way my body seemed to listen to his direction without an ounce of hesitancy wasn't something I was prepared for.

"Beautiful." It was low and seductive; I loved the sound. He reached out to touch me, ran the tip of his finger from my thigh to the underside of my breast. "Exquisite."

"Fuck." The word slipped out on a moan before I could stop it. Camden continued to torture me, slowly; he dragged his finger up and down twice before pulling away.

"Get up on the bed," he hissed through clenched teeth. His hands were balled up tightly at his sides, his nostrils flared, and my pussy throbbed. What the fuck was wrong with me?

I should pull away, put a stop to the madness. It wasn't going to happen. Just the thought of walking out made me feel…off.

All last night I'd prepared myself for what my mother had in store today. It never crossed my mind that I'd meet him. That he would come in to test every brick wall I'd metaphorically put in place to protect myself.

Walking away, I turned to face the bed and took a few steps forward. The table was bare except for the white sheet that lay over the vinyl; there was nothing for me to cover my near-nakedness with.

"What do I cover myself with?"

"You don't."

With both hands placed atop the table, I turned to look at him. He had to be kidding. "Camden, I don't think—"

He stepped closer, almost to the point of touching. "I love the way you say my name. A soft sigh full of desire…need. Say it again."

Shaking my head, I made to turn—his hands reached out to stop me. With both hands on my hips, he lifted me up and onto the table. He maneuvered me, made me feel small and delicate as he placed me to his liking. Face down and ass up.

Camden's strength only ignited a deep-seated yearning I've never felt before. The idea of him taking control over me sexually excited me. While the thought of being a submissive had never crossed my mind—I liked to be dominated in bed.

Hunter had been the only man to touch me like this.

"Amanda," Camden called out, bringing me back to the present and away from a past that would never be. "Pay attention." I nodded. "When in my room, your body and mind are mine. Nothing but what I do to you—for you—matters. I'm the only thing you will hear, see, or smell. Nothing but me." His fingers traveled up from the bottom of my feet to the edge of my panties. I couldn't breathe, and my chest felt tight as I waited on him to proceed. To touch me.

Digging in slightly, he dipped the tip of his fingers under the edge of my panties and pulled back. The hand there trembled as my naked rear came into view.

He let them go; it stung a bit as the material hit my naked flesh. "Do you understand?"

"Yes." I'd signed myself over to him with one word. Camden's ragged breathing gave me comfort; he was just as affected as I was.

"Good." This time, his hands fisted the material with purpose, the tiny scrap of lace stretching. It dug into my hips, and the pain only intensified the moment. My mind was too consumed to protest— to ask him to not ruin the pair I needed to wear later on.

Two tugs were all it took for the flimsy material to give way and tear. The cool air in the room didn't calm my feverish skin; instead, it burned me. Made the raging desires I tried to control enflame into an out-of-control inferno.

Gingerly, his fingers ran soothing circles down my spine. Camden's hands dug in deep for a second before releasing. He never went past my waist, and that frustrated me beyond all reasoning.

"In this room, I want you like this," he whispered before letting a bit of heated oil drip down and pool into the center of my back. "Naked. Open and waiting for what only I can do for you."

"Who says this will happen again?" My taunt didn't faze him.

"I do." The room grew warm then, and my body trembled— spasmed on his table as he spread the heated oil across my back. Camden began applying slight pressure as he pressed his palms down my spine. He would only use his fingers the closer to my ass he got.

Stretching them with each pass, touching more of me.

"That feels so good," I moaned out on one particular upward motion. He'd spread his hands out as he came closer to my ribs. Up his fingers went, massaging and rubbing until they stroked the underside of my breast.

Goosebumps arose. I wanted to turn around and beg him to play with my hardened nipples. As if sensing my thoughts, he pushed me down with one hand on my back while the other ran over my backside.

"Don't rush it. Just feel me."

SEVEN

Amanda

His hands suddenly disappeared.

Frustration was mounting; my thighs were slick, and it wasn't from the oil he'd just barely begun to spread throughout my body. On his table, I was a horny mess of need and want.

Camden did this to me. Messed with everything I knew the moment our eyes met.

"What the…" I'd begun, but his hands—slick and dripping oil on my calves—shut me up. He didn't say a word as he pressed his warm fingers into my flesh. I was pliant in his hands.

Nothing had ever felt so good.

So bad.

So damned right in all my twenty-one years of life.

"Don't move," he groaned, his hands parting my thighs a bit. The cool air inside the room met my wet lips, and I whimpered. "I can smell you."

My response to his words was automatic. Out of my control. "More," I begged and lifted my ass up, offering myself to him.

Camden took in a deep breath, his hands wandering down and

grabbing onto my ass. The tight grip hurt, but felt so good. I never wanted him to stop.

No, I wanted to push him for more.

"Sweetest fucking scent. I bet you taste like sin." He'd squeezed my cheeks, both hands running over the flesh. His fingers were spread, and with each pass, he'd grown bolder, running his thumb around the outside of my wet lips.

"Oh God," I moaned out, his hands stilling for the briefest of seconds before he cupped me. One hand. Camden took me in his hand and pressed into my clit with his palm. "It feels so…"

"I want to fuck you in the worst of ways." He rubbed me. My clit throbbed and pulsed beneath his fingers. "You would let me, too. This pussy," he hissed and entered me with two fingers, "has been aching since I danced with you at Rage. Juicing for my cock."

Maybe I should have been angered by his words, but I wasn't. It had the opposite effect on me—it fueled my need to have him take me. To break his control.

My head rose up and off the table, I wanted to insult him and deny all that he'd just said. But instead, I was stopped by his hand pushing me down at the same time his fingers curled inside of me.

I clenched, my pussy gripped the digits while my thighs squeezed his hands working between them. "*Fuck.*" My sob of pleasure only encouraged him. Camden's hands pushed my legs apart as he began to finger me in earnest. Every nerve ending in my body was crying out for a release. I thrashed as he pushed in deeper, his fingers finding that spot that made me cry.

"I want to feel you come all over my fingers, little *gatita*. Fucking drench me in you." A lone finger caressed me, just on the outside of my labia and gathered the wetness there. "One day, I'm going to stuff my fat cock in both holes, and you will enjoy it."

My mind had gone blank for a second at those words. Wasn't this a one-time deal?

"What do you—" The words died on my tongue. Camden's thumb touched a place no one ever had.

"You'll feel so good wrapped around my cock. Tight and hot—wet and pulsating—as I make you come over and over." It was those words that pushed me. That, and the feel of him playing with my back entrance. He hadn't done more than press down gently, but it was enough to drive me wild.

The tingles ran from the tip of my toes to my clit. I vibrated for him.

"I'm—Motherfuck," I cried out, intense pleasure bursting through me, rocking my body and causing me to push back harder on his finger. Camden's other hand tightened around my ass, kneading the flesh before raising his hand up and down hard against my eager body.

The sting felt euphoric. I undulated harder against his fingers.

"Watching you ride my fingers is a thing of beauty," Camden snarled, and I jumped. He sounded feral, as if he were hanging onto his sanity by a very thin thread. "But nothing compares to your walls pulsating around my fingers. Tight fucking heat. You're a goddamned religious experience."

The scream that erupted from within me was one of agony. Sweetest pain I've ever experienced.

"Shhh, *gatita*," he cooed into my ear as I came down. Camden's fingers never relented; instead, they slowed and prolonged my torture. "You don't want people to hear you, do you? Hear what a dirty kitten you've been. So slutty and wanton for me."

Shaking my head, I pulled my head up and turned to look at him from over my shoulder. "No, you're right, but having Barbie upfront hear me, does sound appealing."

Camden laughed deeply, head thrown back. "You're going to keep me on my toes, aren't you?

I shrugged coyly. "Maybe."

"Please do." He bent down at the waist and kissed my left ass cheek as he pulled his fingers out. "I'll see you next week at three?"

Smiling back at him, I didn't answer. The truth was that I had no clue if I'd be here.

This was all happening too fast for me.

“Hey,” Courtney yelled the moment I walked into the salon. She’d beat me here and was already sitting, hair wet, and being cut. The stylist, an older woman with extremely short hair snipped away, not minding in the least how much her client moved as she waved me down. “How’d it go?”

How was I supposed to answer that? It was great! Best release of my life.

Hell, no. Instead, I smiled and sat beside her. “I haven’t felt this relaxed in ages.”

She arched a brow. “So, he was as good as your mom claimed?” I nodded, but kept quiet. “Hmm, maybe I should make an appointment with him.”

No. Moreover, to that, I’d add a *hell no.*

Over my dead body would she have his hands all over her.

“His schedule seems pretty packed from what I overheard the receptionist tell another client. Instead, she referred her to some other guy she claimed had a few openings. Maybe you can check him out?”

“What aren’t you telling me?” Perceptive bitch was onto me.

“Nothing.” I lied. “Just sharing what I overheard. Plus, she claimed he was a cutie.”

“Okay.” Court looked at me as if I’d lost my head. Sadly, at the moment I had. “Babe, you do remember that I just started seeing someone, right? I don’t think Devin would appreciate you trying to—”

I flipped her off. “I’m not trying to pimp you, woman! Just wanted you to see him and give me your thoughts.”

“Then let me take your slot with Camden—”

“No.” That came out harsher than I intended. “I mean…*fuck*. Just no, Court. Leave it at that for now.”

She looked at me, stared deep into my eyes. Whatever she saw there made her back off. "Fine…"

"Thank you," I sighed and looked up toward the ceiling.

"…For now." Figured as much; I nodded in agreement, never taking my eyes off the white textured surface above.

The following two hours were a blur. I sat there as the stylist worked on me, my mind lost, trying to rationalize everything that'd happened today. When asked what I wanted done, I'd merely mentioned bangs and low lights. Nothing else came to mind; I'd drawn a blank, and it was all Camden's fault. My entire being was just too confused at the moment, consumed by the memories of what I'd just done.

While he cut and textured my layers, I thought of Camden's hands on me and the simple way my body gave itself to him without demanding anything in return.

"Undress for me." Those three words ruined me.

It scared me. Fucking thrilled me. Made me feel and yearn for things I'd never thought twice of in the last few years. Mom, though, she'd dreamed of the day I'd get back together with Hunter and give her grandkids. Funny thing was that she'd sent me to Camden.

She'd also complained about his age. How old was he?

It couldn't be too bad, maybe thirty?

That didn't bother me one bit. No. Not an ounce of concern there.

Maybe it was his long and thick cock that threw me off.

I'd felt his thickness on the dance floor and again today. He'd rubbed himself against my thigh while fingering me, and what pushed against me, could only be described as glorious. The day that I would have him in my hands—bare and warm—would surely kill me.

Then again, my attraction to him wasn't just his cock's girth or length. A dick to fuck isn't something difficult to find in a city like Miami. Men flocked to the bars and clubs my friends frequented on the weekends with that purpose alone. An easy, no-strings-attached night.

That's not something you like. True, but then what? It wasn't his award-winning personality—he barely spoke, but when he did…*Jesus*. Dirty. Explosive. Come-inducing.

His tone, the way he spoke to me, all aroused my inner whore in the most basic of ways. In all the ways a woman wants a man. It was a turn-on.

"Why do you look like you're in pain?" Mom asked, making me jump in my chair much to my stylist's annoyance.

"Quit it." Jeffrey tsked, turning my face forward.

"Sorry," I mumbled and rolled my eyes at my mother.

"Did you not have fun?" Her tone was light, yet her eyes looked too happy. What was she up to now?

Nodding slowly, I looked at her through the mirror. "I'm beyond relaxed. Thank you, Mom."

"I'm so happy to hear you say that, Amanda. Maybe we can make this our…" she pointed between us "…thing on a permanent basis. You know, throw out that whole trial-based clause to our agreement?"

"Getting ahead of yourself there, Susana?"

Her eyes narrowed, and lips pursed. "Watch it, kiddo."

"Give the girl a break, woman." Kimberly stepped in, laughing, while Courtney stood beside her. "By the way, love the bangs. They suit you perfectly, Mandi."

"She is my daughter."

Kim and Courtney stood in front of us with their heads cocked to the side; a mirrored image of the other. Mom looked over at me and bit her lip. We were all beyond ridiculous.

"What the hell does that mean?" Kim broke the stare down.

"Simple," Mom boasted, "she is perfect."

That did it. Everyone around us laughed, including the mother-daughter duo.

"All done," Jeffrey announced, still chuckling at our stupidity. He turned me around then, and I gasped.

It was me.

Just a small bit different.

"I love it." Slowly, I ran my fingers through my straightened locks. Jeffrey had added the low lights, and the darkened tone really stood out against my tanned skin. It meshed beautifully into a chaotic mess of layers that framed my face. The side-swept bangs were fun and made my eyes pop.

"So, you approve?" he hedged, and I laughed. The man did more than just good.

"You rocked it." Jeffrey seemed lost by my reply.

"It means she loved it," Mom explained and began to discuss a hair color change she wanted done. Kim and Courtney had walked off to get something to drink, while I continued to stare into the mirror.

This time, it wasn't myself I was looking at. Camden stood directly behind me on the other side of the salon. He was talking to an older lady, all smiles and laughter. His eyes were set on me, though.

Watching me. Tempting me.

The lady walked away after kissing his cheek, yet he never moved. No, instead his eyes admired me. He mouthed the word "beautiful" twice, and I blushed under his intense scrutiny.

This was beyond inappropriate. Anyone could see our exchange.

I didn't give a flying one anymore.

"Mom?"

"Yes," she answered and turned to look at me. "What is it?"

"We need to do this again, and soon." Consequences be dammed.

EIGHT
Amanda

One week.

One hundred and ninety-two hours.

I didn't even want to think about the number of minutes this equated to. It'd been too long since I had seen him.

Camden hadn't stopped plaguing my mind since we met. How could he, when I was obsessed. I'd close my eyes, and every time, he'd be there smirking at me. Provoking me.

The man was a walking, talking, sculpture of perfection. Beautiful. Not perfect, but a gorgeous man nonetheless. There was a slight bump on his nose; I'd only noticed it when he walked me out of his room. The curve and hump were nothing outrageous; in fact, it was something one might often see in an athlete.

Throughout the last week, I've thought of every scenario where he could've sustained such an injury. I'd even admit to fingering myself to thoughts of him doing these activities. My favorite had him all sweaty and playing soccer with friends.

Muscles rippling as he ran down the field. Chest bared as the sun beat down on him, a trickling of sweat running down the center of his chest and into the waistband of his low-hung shorts.

There was also a small scar over his left brow—a minuscule little thing— that unless you were up close and staring at it, you'd miss it. It was sexy. I'd never wanted to lick a man's eyebrow before.

I was a whimpering mess of infatuation and want for him. It didn't sit well with me.

Never had I lusted after a man like this, especially after being in his presence for less than a few hours. Hate and want. Crazy emotions swirled within me, mixed with shame. What we did was reckless.

He could lose his job and I, my dignity.

It's not your dignity you're worried about. No. It wasn't. If things went further, I had no doubt that he would destroy my heart.

Was this the norm for him? Did he sleep or touch all clients so intimately?

I banged my head against the kitchen table.

Everything from his eyes to his slightly crooked nose made him beautiful to me. It gave him that extra edge that all men wanted and very few achieved.

I wanted to go back. Now. Yesterday. The very minute we walked out of the hotel and back into the car, but I couldn't. Not yet, or it would be too obvious.

"Pick up your phone, kiddo," Dad complained as he entered the kitchen and pulled a bottle of water out of the fridge. "It's been going off nonstop for the last ten minutes. That god-awful ringtone you love so much has been blaring on a constant loop."

"Huh?" That was an eloquent reply if I'd ever heard one.

He watched me; eyebrow raised and rubbed his chin. "What's got you in a funk?"

"Nothing."

"And I'm the king of Spain." He pulled a chair up beside me. Elbows on the table, face in his hands, he watched me. It was unnerving. The man knew me better than I did most days. "Again, what has you looking like that? Sad?"

I shrugged and looked down at the magazine before me. "I'm not sad, Dad, just trying to piece together something that makes no sense. You know, like a puzzle that's missing parts and no matter what you try to replace it with, it still makes no sense."

"Whose butt do I have to beat?" Member of the city council or not, he's always been protective of me. Sometimes excessive, but it was all due to his love.

"No *one's,* old man." I nudged his shoulder with mine. "Just—"

It rang again, I picked it up and looked at the caller ID with confusion. This wasn't a number I knew.

"Well," Dad hedged while standing up to leave. "Aren't you going to answer it?"

It stopped ringing before I could. I opened my mouth, just barely saying the words "I was," when it rang again. Same number. Still private.

This time, I stood up and walked toward the patio doors, away from the nosy old man, and answered it on the third ring. The warm sun felt spectacular on my face.

Looking up, I closed my eyes and took in a deep breath. "Hello."

"About fucking time, *gatita*."

"Camden?" I choked out.

His chuckle was low, rough. "Expecting someone else?"

"Maybe." He didn't laugh. There was no way I could continue to let him have the upper hand. Enough. "Was there something you needed?"

"You." There was so much frustration and anger laced through that one word.

"What the hell—"

"Why weren't you here today?" It was an accusation.

"What do you mean?" He wasn't explaining. None of this made sense.

"Amanda," Camden hissed low, "don't play games with me. You weren't here. Why?"

Hearing him. Sensing his desire did things to my depraved mind. He wanted more from me than the one-time fingering.

"I wasn't aware I had an appointment," I cooed into the phone. "Please forgive me."

"Every Wednesday at three, I expect you in my room. No excuses."

"And if I can't or am otherwise obligated elsewhere?" My unoccupied hand fisted my hair and tugged slightly, just as he had last week. It stung, and I gasped.

"I don't give a flying fuck what you are doing. Where the hell are you?" Another accusation. The man demanded much more than he gave.

"Does it matter where or with whom?" I was pulling the lion's tail, but I wanted his bite.

"Mark my words, that cute little ass of yours will be tinged pink by the time we are through next week." My nipples hardened at his words.

The words, *yes, sir* sat on the very tip of my tongue.

Instead of letting him hear the desperation he caused, I gave him lip. "Is this how you treat all your clients? Do you sleep with every one of them?"

"What I do or—"

"Answer me," I spit out through clenched teeth, while walking further out into the backyard. The last thing I needed was for my parents to hear this conversation. "Answer or I hang up. Simple as that."

"No." His one-word answers were beginning to get on my nerves.

Taking in a deep breath did nothing to help calm my mounting frustration. "That isn't an answer."

"It is, just not the one you want."

"You're right." I pulled the phone from my ear and hit the end button. It hurt to disconnect. Physically hurt me. The phone rang again, but I never answered. It rang repeatedly. Screw him for making this harder.

I turned back toward the house, my mind made up on letting this crazy thing go when it pinged instead. He was a player, and I'd fallen into his trap. The entire situation sucked, but it was best that I knew now.

Looking down, I swiped my finger across the screen and opened my text messages, thinking it was Court. It wasn't. Why couldn't he let me be?

I'm sorry. Please come next Wednesday at three…I'll explain. No more bullshit. ~Cam

My response was quick. Unlike him, I wasn't playing games. All I needed from him was to know what this was and if we were to continue, that his cock wasn't massaging anyone else.

I'll think about it. ~Mandi

Fair enough, and wear something white. Only white. ~Cam

SAYING I WAS A NERVOUS WRECK WOULD BE THE UNDERSTATEMENT of the century as I pulled into the hotel's valet parking. It was rather empty, only one car before me.

The muffler was loud, a special little upgrade Dad wanted to add. The sexy hum of power made the parking attendants turn and rush over to me. They didn't care one bit about the older lady in front of me sitting in her Cadillac.

I let them open my door, even handed the same kid that had eye fucked my mom the keys without a word. He got in and slammed the door closed; I didn't even bat an eyelash.

Entering the warmly decorated hotel lobby didn't make me smile this time. To any stranger on the street, I looked to be in pain. A sexual pain, if I were to be honest.

The Spa's name came into view the further inside I walked. My heart beat fast. Palms became sweaty.

Fuck, I wasn't ready.

Ready to hear lies or his hurtful truths. This could go either way, but only one viable possibility stood out. I'd be hurt either way.

"Are you heading inside, Miss?" It was the same older lady with the Cadillac standing before me. "You okay?"

"To be honest…" I chuckled humorlessly "…I'm not sure how to answer that."

"You're looking a little pale, sweetie. Why don't we head over to the little café and get something to drink? I have thirty minutes before I'm due for my cut and color."

Nodding, I walked beside her while we strolled across the lobby. The small shop she'd mentioned was really a gift shop that sold cold beverages and cheesy Miami souvenirs. Grabbing a Coke for me and a diet for herself, she batted my hands away when I tried to pay.

"My treat."

I huffed with a smile on my face. The old lady was cool. "Are you sure?"

"Yes, now grab these, and sit down on the couch over there and wait." Did I mention a bit pushy too?

Once she came back, we chatted for a bit. Nothing serious. Just the basics, like the weather, and how no matter what time of year it was in Miami, it was hot as hell. Her words, not mine.

We drank our sodas, and by the time she stood to leave, I felt better. At the very least, I would have my answers.

"All right, dear, it's already 3:10. We need…" I didn't hear the rest of what she'd said. My mind was too busy circulating over two words. I'm late. Giving her a quick hug and kiss on the cheek, I grabbed my drink and rushed toward the entrance.

It was just in sight, the name standing bright. Not brighter than he, though.

Camden stood in all his pissed-off, sexy glory by the door, a scowl on his face, arms crossed over his chest. His eyes—those beautiful eyes were a raging sea of ire as he watched me rush toward him.

"You're late."

"I know, but—" He placed a single finger over my lips. I wanted to lick that tip. Bite it.

"First rule. Never make me wait for you. You won't like the consequences of defying that major commandment."

"You aren't in any real position to threaten me, Camden. Push me too far, and I'll walk."

His eyes slowly perused my body, a low hum of approval leaving his throat. "Bullshit."

"Excuse me?" Cocking my hip to the side, I placed my hand there and glared. This cocky asshole didn't know me.

"I said…*bullshit.*" Camden's smirk grew; his lopsided and beautiful little smile had me pressing my thighs closer together. He pulled off the wall and stood right in front of me. The anger was still there, it simmered, but he seemed more entranced by my appearance than the reason I made him wait.

Arching my brow, I waved him on. "Explain."

"Easy." Closer still. Chest slightly touching mine as he breathed me in. "You wore this for me; this all white and small tight dress. Nipples pebbling and brushing against the material as your breathing gets labored the closer I get. For me."

"I don't—"

"Bet your pussy's wet."

"Are you insane?" I whisper yelled. People were walking all around us. Some looking. Most didn't give a flying one.

"Since I met you? Yes." We were nose to nose now. His breath brushed over my face, and instinctually I licked my lips. A movement he followed with his eyes.

"You're driving me insane."

He swallowed hard, his eyes were heavy with lust. "You make me want to fuck myself into your system. Somewhere you can't erase my cock from your memory. Where you'll feel me with every breath you take."

"Camden, I—"

Placing a finger over my lips, he traced them softly. "Not another word, gatita. Inside. Now."

NINE
Amanda

"Undress for me."

The door hadn't fully closed when he uttered my instructions. It wouldn't cut it today. Not after everything he'd said in our last conversation. All the questions he'd promised to answer.

"No." Turning his way, I leaned back against the table's edge and regarded him with my bitchiest expression. "I have some questions for you. Answer them, and then I'll play."

"I've already said all I had to say. Wasn't I clear enough outside?" He was annoyed by my reluctance to play his way. "Enough time has been wasted, and I'll need more than the remaining hour to get my fill of you."

I shook my head and arched a brow. "Again, no."

Camden ran a frustrated hand down his face. "Why are you being so difficult?"

"Why are you evading this thing between us?" I countered, arms crossed over my chest. Was it such a bad thing to admit there was something happening between the two of us?

Shit. Was he married? Seeing someone?

The last two almost made me ill. How could I have been so blind and stupid?

He took an angry step closer. His hypnotizing male scent hit me full force, like the sea and the pure essence of sex collided. *Fuck* if it didn't make me shiver.

"Cold?" Camden chuckled. His hand reached out to uncross my arms, but I ducked away. His brow scrunched up in confusion, and a brief flash of hurt passed through his eyes. "What's gotten—"

"Are you married?" I blurted out, interrupting him. Taken aback, he took a few steps back, to his original post in front of the door. If I wasn't sure that the cocky bastard didn't care, I'd say he was afraid I'd leave.

"No. I'm not." *Okay.* "There isn't a girlfriend either, *gatita.* I'm by no means a saint, but a fucking cheater I am not." My body physically relaxed at those words. The earlier tightness in my chest lessened to the point the next breath I took didn't hurt. "What about you, Amanda? Is there someone I should be concerned with?" There went that accusatory tone again. "Not that it'd matter much. Nothing will stop me when it comes to you." Camden's jaw was set hard. It ticked with anger, and his eyes glared. He intimidated me.

"Not for a long time. No."

"Good." His stiff posture loosened a bit. "Undress." Goddamned, frustrating asshole. The game he played was driving me insane. I was confused, angry—a horny wet whore for him.

"What are we doing here, Camden? This isn't me. I'm just not the casual finger or fuck type of girl."

He smiled. Not a cocky smirk or a know-it-all smile. It was soft and sincere. "I know."

That's it. Two words, and they said more to me than any lengthy speech would.

"Then, what's going on? Why do you need me here every Wednesday at three?"

"Because I'm an asshole, *gatita.*" Camden's breathing sped up. "I don't do relationships. Not since my divorce three years ago. Casual was working fine until I saw you in that fucking club sitting all prim and proper. I wanted to corrupt you the moment we breathed the same air."

"And now?" I whispered, pushing off the table. My feet carried me to him, chest to fucking chest. Our breaths mingled between us. "Now what?"

"Now, I want to take with no regard. Say a big 'fuck you' to what's right—appropriate." He reached out tentatively and cupped my face in his hands. "Would you let me? Take until I've gorged myself? Until my cock's raw from fucking you, and even then, let me have you again?"

Nuzzling the palm of his hand, I kissed it and turned my eyes to his. "I don't share. I'm an all-or-nothing kind of girl."

"No sharing for me either." He tipped my face up to his and nipped my bottom lip. "The thought of anyone else…"

Sighing deep, I pulled his hands from my face and kissed the tip of his finger. "Exclusive means relationship, Camden. It's either you want this, or you don't."

"How about we enjoy this and see where it goes. No labels for now."

Could I do that? Trust him?

Would he be truthful and only see me?

I'd have to. There was no other choice left for me. Not seeing *him* was out of the question. The mere thought of walking away made me feel off.

Standing on the tip of my toes, I kissed him. The way I took his mouth was hard and punishing. Raw need exploded within me at the taste of him on my tongue.

I nipped his bottom lip once and pulled back. "Yes."

"Thank you—"

"For now." I cut him off, pressing my finger to his lips. He smiled and nodded, pulling me in closer.

And I meant it, too. I'd give him space, but eventually, this non-status-label bull would have to change.

He liked me, yet fought against what felt natural. What was instinctual.

I turned around then, letting the heat from his body sear my back. He dominated the space and made me forget everything but the length of his cock rubbing against me.

Everything else disappeared. Our talk. My wants. Nothing but his hardness mattered.

Thick and hard—hot.

"Can I undress now?"

Desperation colored my tone. Yearning. Hunger. It was all there as I begged him to play with me. To manipulate my body to his liking.

The urgent growl that passed through his lips made me squeak. It was ferocious and deep, that of an animal on the hunt that's caught the scent of its favorite prey.

Camden's nimble fingers ran up the base of my spine. They wandered every inch until he found the knot that held my simple cotton dress in place at the base of my neck. It was all that held me covered from him. Easy access in every sense of the word.

"Thank you," he groaned, spinning me around to face him. His lips met mine with urgency, the kiss felt almost reverent, as if he wanted to drown in my taste. "Have I told you how beautiful you look today?" I shook my head and pressed my lips harder against his. "You do. All in white like a good little girl. It's maddening in the best of ways."

"Just following instructions," I whispered into his mouth.

"Baby," he growled as the knot gave way and the simple cotton fabric began to fall down. It pooled between us, his chest and mine stopping its descent to the floor.

"You like?" My hips pressed into his, trapping his dick between us as I swiveled against him, massaging the hardened length that pulsed against me.

"You're a goddamned innocent temptation. Little she-devil dressed in white and dripping innocence. You're driving me to the edge of madness." Camden spat the words with false disdain. One hand held the back of my neck, the grip tight.

It was exciting. There was nothing sexier to me than being manipulated by this man.

I wanted more.

"I'm not that innocent, Camden." It was a taunt, a dare that someone else had been between my thighs. "You aren't my first, nor do you scare me."

"Don't push me." The hand he'd just placed on my hip tightened. Hard. The anger and yearning that stared back at me made me gasp. Fucking shook me to the core.

"I'm—"

"When I'm through with you, it will be my hips imprinted on your thighs. It will be my cock that you mourn when I pull out, and the memory of us—in this room—that you cry out for at night when you miss me." The wetness I'd tried so hard to ignore ran down my thighs. His nostrils flared, and he took in a deep breath. "You fucking like that, don't you? The thought of feeling me for days after?"

"Yes." It was the truth. This was wrong, crazy—a goddamned mistake, yet it also felt right in every sense of the word. "I want you."

Camden pushed down my dress before picking me up and carrying me over to his table. We were both past the point of rationalizing and needed to feel the other urgently. He laid me on the edge and stood between my parted thighs, eyeing with contempt the small piece of lace that hid me from him.

"I'm sorry." Leaning over me, he kissed my lips sweetly while fisting the small lace panties I wore. The material stretched. They dug into me as he tore them from my body.

"Shit." I hissed out and bit down on his lip hard enough to draw the tiniest bit of blood. His responding groan was sexy. Camden appreciated a little pain.

"*Fuck*, yeah." He stood up and wiped his lip, traces of my lip gloss still on him. Camden stared; his eyes raped me before looking up at the clock on the wall. "We only have twenty minutes left. Nowhere near enough time for me to fuck you, devour your goddamned perfection."

"You can't leave me like this!"

"Hush, *gatita.*" Humming, his hand reached out to cup my jaw and squeezed once before letting go. Those same fingers then tapped my lips. "Open."

I did. Everything, even just talking was exhilarating with him. New. Fresh. Sexy.

With his other hand, he placed the same white panties I'd worn today just inside my mouth, barely sitting between my lips and teeth.

"Don't drop them. You do, and I'll stop." The rush of wetness that fell down the crack of my ass made me feel embarrassed. My clit pulsed, trembled, and he'd yet to touch me.

Looking up, I spied the clock and saw we only had fifteen minutes left. "Camden," I complained around the lace, "the…oh shit!" He'd lost his pants and now stood before me, cock in hand. His thick, fucking glorious manhood had me salivating. A clear drop of liquid sat at the tip and rolled down the length. "Let me feel you on my tongue." He shook his head, denying me. "Please."

"No." The one hand not holding his length pried my legs farther apart. He stepped closer and eyed the wetness leaving my pussy with thirst. "But I will be taking one small taste."

Camden bent at the waist and ran the flat of his tongue from the bottom of my slit to my engorged clit. I trembled and screamed, the sound muffled by the small panties in my mouth. My teeth bit down hard into the makeshift gag.

"One lick will never be enough. Sweetest temptation divine." His lips wrapped around my clit—sucking, licking. He flicked his tongue against the swollen bundle of nerves, and I arched off the table. My lips opened, the moan of pleasure caught in my throat.

"Don't drop them, or I will stop." Camden's words did nothing to help center me. I was already half gone to the sensations he created. Taking one long, last lick, he pulled back and watched me. My wetness on his lips caused my hips to buck up. It was me he inhaled in deep and licked off those juicy lips.

"More," I shamelessly begged.

Again, he shook his head. This time, though, he took a step closer. Close enough to let me savor his heat against my bare pussy.

"I'll make you come, *gatita*, but this time I'll get mine too. Let me paint your skin with my essence."

I was confused for about two seconds until he tapped the head of his cock against my clit. Three times in rapid succession he slapped me there, where I trembled for him. The grunt of pleasure he drew from me was raw.

Almost hurt.

"Yes. Fuck, Camden!" The panties fell from between my teeth and onto the table beneath me. He didn't even notice. He was relentless. His cockhead met my clit with a mixture of hard taps and soft caresses.

"Five minutes, *gatita*." He pushed two fingers inside me and left them there as he rubbed himself all over my wetness. "Are you close?" I nodded and pushed up against him. The fingers inside my pussy anchored me. He twisted them up and at the same time smacked my swollen red lips with his entire cock.

"Fuck. Again, *gatita*. Let me feel that clit quiver against my dick." That was it. He pumped his fingers inside me while alternating between rubbing and tapping. It drove me over. The sensations were too much.

I buried my fingers in his hair and pulled. "Don't stop."

"Come, goddammit!" He pulled his fingers out and placed the head of his dick at my entrance. "I'm so close, baby."

Pushing myself up, I stared down at where he held himself. "Do it."

"Want to fuck you so bad," he groaned and pushed just the tip in. "So hot."

"What's stopping you," I taunted. Wrapping my legs around him, I pulled him closer. Camden stopped, just held himself inside, and stared me down. The lust and want reflected in his eyes caused my own to roll back. "Take me."

In one smooth stroke, he was inside of me. One thrust, and the world around me shifted.

I came. No other way to explain what happened, but I let go and welcomed the euphoric feel of him twitching inside me to take me under.

"Fucking perfection. I feel you…squeeze me, dammit!" Camden hissed and slammed back in. Hips flush against mine; he gyrated and pushed in harder. The harshness of his movements was in desperation. As if he wanted to go in deeper. Become a part of me.

"Need to feel you, Camden. Come on me." Our eyes locked, he nodded, and then pulled out. I missed his warmth immediately.

"I'm going to paint my ownership on your pussy. Fuck that…my *gatita*." Fisting himself, he stood over me and pumped his cock. Up and down in harsh tugs, fist tight and twisting on the upstroke.

Wanting to push him further, my hand wandered down my torso. Fingers caressed my mound before dipping low and over my clit. I was sensitive and still turned on beyond all comprehension.

"Come, Camden. Please, baby." His eyes followed the movement of my fingers, punishing himself until his eyes rolled back and he sprayed the first jet of come on my stomach. "So hot."

He looked down then and bit his lip. Watching how the second stream landed right above my clit. How it dribbled down and mixed with my own juices.

"How will I ever let you go?" It was spoken aloud, but I doubted he was aiming that at me. Instead, he continued to pump and watch as the last two spurts landed on my clit and lips. I wore him, and he loved every single minute of it. "Beautiful."

Camden didn't move until he'd emptied the last drop. Even then, he stood and watched, sometimes running his fingers up and down my lips, combining our juices.

"You know that our time is up, right?" Quirking a brow, I waited for him to move so I could go and clean up.

He shrugged and continued to play. “I’m not ready for you to go.”

“What about your next appointment?” Truth was, I wasn’t ready to let him go either. It was a dangerous game we played, but I needed this time alone with him. These minutes made me feel less like a dirty little secret.

“I cleared my schedule for you. No rush. Just let me enjoy you a little more.” He’d lied to me about how much time we’d had left.

I wanted to be annoyed at him. Even tried, but I couldn’t.

There was too much delight at the idea of him surprising me like this, making room to spend time with me in his schedule.

I’d be a fool to say no.

TEN

Amanda

After we cleaned up, once Camden was through having fun pushing his come inside my body, we walked out toward the lobby.

"Mandi?" I stopped dead in my tracks, my back colliding with Camden's front as the familiar voice said my name again. It was once the voice that made me smile, that made everything better in my world. "Hey, beautiful."

"Hunter?" Turning around, I faced my past with my hopeful future beside me. Never in a million years did I think we'd find ourselves in the same room again. Back in the same city as me. "What are you doing here?"

Hunter looked perplexed by my question. "Didn't Susana tell you I work here now?"

Things made sense now. Mom's insistence that I come and be massaged here specifically. How her eyes were bright as she told me I would love what I'd find. That conniving little shit.

Why? She was witness to how heartbroken I was when he left for school. How I tried to reason with him that we could make a long-distance relationship work.

"I'm sorry, Hunter, but she didn't." Shaking my head, I took a step closer, only to be pulled back. Right back into Camden's tense form. The heat of his anger fell over me like a scorching blanket. His breathing was harsh against the back of my head, and his fingers tightened their hold.

It was a silent dare to move forward again.

Hunters hazel eyes left mine and moved over to Camden's. They hardened, taking in how close we were. How Camden shifted his body with mine with each move I made.

"Hey, Cam," Hunter greeted and ran an agitated hand through his black hair, the cheery tone fake and the polite smile forced. "I didn't know you were the therapist seeing my girl."

What the hell was he doing? My life wasn't a game.

"I am." He was shutting down on me. I could sense the immediate change in how quickly he released the hold he had on my dress. The minute step he'd taken back.

"Hunter, I'm your ex, not your current. Remember, you made that choice two years ago." Camden's chuckle behind me was anything but quiet.

Hunter turned to fully face him and glared. "What's so funny, Daniels?"

"Watch it, kid," Camden hissed and pulled me behind him. "Today's not the day to push your luck with me—I won't be stopped." Whoa. What the hell?

"Guys, stop it!" Their eyes snapped back to mine, possessive anger shining through both sets of orbs. They needed to be separated before someone threw a punch.

"Why is he standing so close to you, Mandi?" Hunter growled, trying to reach around Camden's menacing form and grab my arm. Wrong fucking move.

Before I could respond or pull back, Camden slammed him against the opposite wall from me, his forearm pressed tightly against Hunter's neck. "Don't fucking touch her."

"Camden!" I yelled out and grabbed onto the back of his shirt. He didn't move, only shrugged me away and with one dirty look, dared me to try that again. "Please stop. For fuck's sake, we're in public! I'm surprised no one's walked back here to see what's going on."

"Get off me," Hunter snarled, pushing against the hold Camden had on him. Camden didn't move an inch, not even when Hunter's elbow connected with his ribs.

It didn't seem to faze him one bit.

My first instinct was to pull his shirt up and see the damage. My fingers twitched to make sure he was okay. Camden's hard eyes kept me in place. They told me that now was not the time.

"He shouldn't touch what doesn't belong to him." Each word dripped with venom. As the last word left Camden's lips, he pushed himself off and grabbed my hand. "She's of-limits, Hunter."

"The fuck she is." Hunter had a death wish. The muscles in Camden's arms flexed, and his hands were balled into tight fists. The man was trying to control himself. "I came back to reclaim whats mine, and no one…" he jabbed his finger into Camden's chest "… will stop me."

Camden eyed the finger on his chest. He looked at it with amusement before his arm cocked back and he connected with the side of Hunter's face. *Holy shit!*

The sad part was that I felt nothing as Hunter's head snapped to the side. Not even when he hit the wall behind him. Not a damn thing.

Where there once was love sat the possibility of friendship, but now, his idiotic behavior killed all prospects of any type of relationship. Hunter was no longer a part of my life, and he never would be again.

"Are you out of your mind?" We were going to be thrown out of this place. They were acting like five-year-olds fighting over their favorite toy. "Get up and leave, Hunter."

"What? You're picking his side?" He had the nerve to act indignant.

"You brought this shit upon yourself. Act like an ass, get knocked out like one." Camden laughed beside me, his murderous eyes stilled locked on Hunter's stumbling form.

At this, I turned and glared at Camden. "Shut it."

He ignored me, and then surprised me with a tender kiss on my cheek. "Hungry?"

Camden didn't wait for my reply—instead, he grabbed my hand and entwined our fingers together. We walked past a still fuming Hunter. We almost made it to the door when he spoke again.

"I'll see you later tonight, Mandi."

"What are you talking about?" Did the hit knock the sense right out of him? Why continue pushing Camden? Hunter was not blind; he could see we were in some sense of the word "together."

"Susana invited me over for dinner tonight." His expression was smug, as if he'd won this round.

Camden pulled me closer, ignoring the blatant jab. "I'll be sure to release her in time for the glorious event."

"So..." we both began. We'd just sat down at a small hole-in-the-wall sandwich shop in the middle of downtown and neither knew where to begin. Camden looked uncomfortable, and I wasn't in any better shape.

He cleared his throat and stared me down. His facial expression told me nothing of how he felt. Instead, his indifference made me nervous. Made me wonder just what was going on behind those beautiful eyes.

"Just ask." Impatience colored my tone. We were both waiting for our food and at a loss. Camden had questions and I the answers. "Nothing's off the table."

"He's the ex." It wasn't a question. "Never—"

"Never what?" In all honesty, I knew where his mind had gone. Hunter was a dick, and while I wasn't blind to it in the past, now his faults felt like an embarrassment to me.

"Hunter didn't deserve you then, and I'll be fucked if he has you now." Those words, as simple as they were, made me smile. Who knew the smug bastard could be sweet?

"Thank you." What else could I say? It was the truth.

"How long were you with him?" The waitress took that moment to deliver our food. Her eyes lingered on Camden; wandering down his face and onto his chest while licking her lips.

"Can I get you anything else?" Amy—as her name tag read—simpered while placing our lunch on the small table. My first reaction was annoyance, but then I remembered that I had no claim on Camden, and that hurt.

I watched his face as she flirted. Watched him smile and decline her offer. The sudden tightness in my chest lessened, but didn't disappear. How long would I put up with this shit?

"Why do you look pissed?" Camden reached over the table and ran his fingertips across my cheekbone. "Is it because of..." he waved his hand in the waitress's direction.

"No."

"Bullshit, and you know it."

"Leave it alone, Camden." He ignored me and stood up from the table abruptly. His chair scraped against the cheap linoleum flooring, causing the few other patrons in the place to look our way.

"Look at me." My eyes met his angry ones as I let him pull me out of my seat. We stood close. So close I could almost taste the mango from his smoothie. "I'm here with you. Not her, or any other piece of ass at the moment, *gatita*. Cut the jealousy act out."

You have got to be kidding me.

"So let me get this straight." I paused and looked at him coolly. "You can pull the jealous 'don't touch what's mine' crap on me, but I can't look displeased because she practically offered her crotch on a platter?"

"Amanda," he began, annoyance tinging his tone. I wasn't having any of it. I'd let Hunter call the shots during the entire length of our relationship, and I'd be damned if I'd do it with Camden.

"I'll see you next week." I tried to pull my hand from his grasp, but he didn't budge. Instead, he secured the other around my waist.

"You're not leaving. Fuck, no," he snarled, lips pressed harshly against mine. "You, my dear *gatita*, will sit down and listen to what I have to say."

"Let me go." Camden ignored my hiss of displeasure, and after nipping my lip once, pushed me back down to sit. He moved his chair beside mine. Our knees touched, and his hand laid claim to my exposed thigh.

The simple contact made me shiver. The ripple of pleasure caused me to stiffen beside him.

"Amanda, I like you, and I won't deny that there is something happening between us." My eyes met his. The hardness they held a few minutes prior had dissipated, and what was left made me feel uncomfortable. I saw what he was going to say in those deep eyes before he uttered the next syllable.

"There will never be an us, will there?"

Sadly, he shook his head. "No. I'm not looking for a relationship, Amanda. It's not in the cards for me." The words stung, but I knew this was his truth deep down.

"Then why…" I cleared my throat, trying in vain to dislodge the sudden invisible knot of emotions making me choke up. "Why get territorial? Hunter—"

"Don't say his fucking name." The grip he had on my thigh tightened, not to hurt or bruise, but enough to let me feel his displeasure. I tried to pry his fingers away, but he wouldn't be moved.

"You can't do that. I am no one's plaything."

"No one said that you—"

"I wasn't finished." He waved me on while ignoring the glare I was sending his way. "You can't choose when to care or act like a jilted lover at the mention of another's name. It's not fair."

"Hunter doesn't deserve you."

The snort that passed through my lips couldn't be stopped. "Who the hell are you to have an opinion on the matter? We are nothing, remember?"

"I know." The words were spoken so low I almost didn't hear them. Turbulent eyes met mine, and they asked for understanding. "I know I have no right, but I can't just walk away. It isn't an option for me."

Sighing, I grabbed his hand on my thigh and squeezed. "So, how the hell is this supposed to work, because for some reason the thought of walking away bothers me. I'm as helpless as you are in this mess."

"Fucked if I know." I laughed at his grumpy reply. What was I thinking getting myself wrapped up in this catastrophe, because it was sure to end as one? "I haven't had a relationship since my divorce."

"How long has it been?"

"Three glorious years." Camden's answer threw me for a loop. Was he that against being in a monogamous relationship?

"Explain."

He scratched the short scruff on his jaw and watched my expression. "Not much to explain, really. We married young—she was all I knew, and I hated her for that. My life at that moment was dictated by our relationship. She lived her life while I was fucked over and was deprived pussy in return."

With those few words, he destroyed a tiny part of my attraction to him. He reminded me of Hunter and the words he said to me before he left. All that mattered to them was having someone to fuck.

I love you, Mandi, but I need more. To explore what's out there without worrying about you or us. I'm sorry, but I'm leaving us behind when I get to New York.

"Are you listening to me?" He waved a hand across my face, snapping me back to the present.

"Sorry," I spoke low and pulled a little bit away. The space was needed for me to clear the conflicted thoughts he created. "What were you saying?"

"We met in high school and started dating our sophomore year. She was sweet. Beautiful and fun. After graduation is where the problems began. She wanted to stay here and I wanted to join the Air Force. She hated the idea of us separating, and I understood because I was committed to her."

"So what happened?" Grabbing my soda, I took a sip while trying to digest what he was trying to make me see.

"I stayed." His facial expression was soft, sincere. "At first, it was okay. We moved in together and were happy. She went to FIU while I took a job at The Ritz doing maintenance to keep us afloat. While she partied, I worked and came home tired."

"Didn't she work to help out?" Shaking his head, he reached out and pulled me closer, terminating the space I'd created between us.

"No, Olivia didn't work…she didn't cook or clean either. It was all on me, and I resented her for that." In a sense, I could understand where he was coming from. Camden had been the giver and she took advantage, creating the man before me.

"How long did it last?" Without meaning to, my hand reached out and caressed his cheek. He nuzzled the palm and then kissed it.

"Six years. For six years I put up with her neediness. Her immaturity. I was done, and on our anniversary served her with the divorce papers." You could feel the bitterness in his tone. While he may not love her, she left her mark for the rest of us to try and erase.

The question now was: did I want to try and change his mind?

As the conversation progressed, we had pulled closer. Our foreheads touched and our eyes spoke what neither said.

"How did she take it?" I whispered and kissed his lips once. A soft peck.

"She was relieved, said she had fallen in love with someone else." What a fucking bitch. "Olivia used me, and I vowed after my divorce to never put myself in that position again."

"Okay. I accept your explanation, and I'll even take it into consideration while making up my mind concerning us."

Camden's eyebrows knit together and his lips pursed. "What's that supposed to mean?"

"It means…" I laughed dryly "…that while I understand, I don't accept. I'm not her, and I refuse to pay for her stupidity."

"Amanda—"

Placing my finger over his lips, I cut him off. "I'm not done, Camden. You have your reasons, and while they are valid, I'll never be your booty call."

"I'm not asking you to." He slammed his hand down on the table, causing me to jump and pull back. The couple a few tables over looked at us, but I waved their concern away. "You're running before walking."

"Then what are you asking of me?" He was purposely trying to confuse me, and I didn't appreciate it. "Be clear here. No more games."

"Who says I'm asking you for anything?"

Fuck this. I stood up from the table then and leaned toward him. The sudden movement caught him off guard, and a small flash of uncertainty flashed across his face.

"Right now," I sneered while fisting his locks, "you remind me of him. Hunter's an asshole, and you're quickly earning the same title." He went to speak, but I silenced him with a fierce kiss. I took everything he didn't want to give me with that one kiss. Camden wanted me, it was all there in the way he groaned at my taste. How his hands reached out to always pull me closer. He had no choice. "You're on borrowed time, baby. Change my mind." With that, I pushed him back in his seat and walked out the door.

Let him make of that whatever he wanted.

ELEVEN
Amanda

I drove around the city after leaving Camden.

So many emotions surged through me: confusion, anger, and at the end acceptance. Was the acceptance over the category he'd put me under? Not sure, but at the very least, I knew where I stood with him. It was up to me to continue or walk away.

Then there was my mother. How could she, for even a minuscule of a second, entertain the idea I'd want Hunter back? Not in this lifetime or the next would that be possible.

You don't purposely hurt what you claim to love.

"Mandi, is that you?" Mom called out from the living room as soon as I entered through the garage. She sounded happy and upbeat. Hunter was already here if the unknown car in our driveway was anything to go by.

Sighing, I threw my keys on the counter and walked through the hallway toward the formal living room. They all sat there. All three looked up as I entered.

"Honey, look who came by to see you?" Mom's smile was huge, all teeth and eyes shining.

"I see." The smile fell from her face at my bitter response. Good.

Maybe she'd realize how much of an uncomfortable situation she'd put me in.

Looking over at Dad, he was smiling at me with sympathy in his eyes and shaking his head. The action spoke volumes to me. He wasn't happy with Hunter's presence and only tolerated this because of my mother.

"Amanda." My eyes snapped back to hers. "Aren't you going to say hello to our guest?"

An exasperated chuckle passed through my lips. "Do I have a choice in the matter or is this your way of telling me I need to?"

"Young lady—"

"Save it," I snapped, and she recoiled. I'd never raised my voice to her, but this was beyond parenting. She'd meddled. Thought she could decide for me, and on this, I wouldn't back down.

I felt betrayed and rightfully so.

"Mandi, respect." Dad's voice was firm and left no room for argument. "I understand you're upset—"

"Bruce!"

"Susana, let me finish." Mom sat back against the couch with a huff. "She has every right to be upset when you bring…" he pointed an angry finger at Hunter "…this man into our home. You should've asked her, not assumed that she'd be happy. Don't forget that he left her."

"Mr. Brooks, I know that I screwed up, but I love her." Did Hunter think his words would simplify his actions? Love? Fuck his love. His actions in the past spoke louder than any declaration ever could.

I rolled my eyes at his audacity. "No, you don't."

"Mandi, can we please go outside and talk? Please. Just hear me out, and then I'll leave." My head was shaking in a negative when Mom jumped in and answered for me.

"She'd love to, and you're staying for dinner...right?" What the hell?

"Susana, enough!" Dad stood up and yelled. We were all shocked

—he never yelled, much less at her. "You will not push her—don't forget who you should be loyal to out of the two."

"I just want her happy," she snapped back. "Don't you remember how good they were together? What's wrong with wanting my little girl to have what I have with you?"

This was quickly getting out of hand. Fighting wasn't the norm in this house, and it was all due to the stupid prick sitting on the couch smiling at me.

"Enough," I seethed while walking up to Hunter. "You should leave. There's nothing for you here."

His smile dropped, and his eyes narrowed. "Is there someone else?"

My parents ceased their arguing and turned to look at me. How do I explain that there is, but isn't? That in reality, I have no clue if continuing to see Camden would be a good thing.

I pointed my finger in Hunter's smug face. "Not that it's any of your business, but yes."

"Who? Why haven't you told me?" Mom gasped and took a tentative step toward me. Her tone held curiosity and mild recrimination. As if I owed her this information.

"You want the honest truth?" She nodded and waited for my reply while I turned to face her. Nothing sucked more than having to hurt your parents' feelings, but she needed to face reality. I was an adult and should be respected. "It isn't any of your business."

"What's gotten into you?" Her hand reached out to grasp my shoulder, but I took a step back.

"How about the fact that you thought bringing him into my home would be okay? Or maybe the fact that you are so desperate to see us together that you never cared if this would hurt me?"

"Mandi, don't be so hard on her—" Hunter began, but my angry glare cut him off.

"Outside, now." Turning away from Hunter, I walked up to Dad and kissed his cheek. "I'll be a minute."

"You sure, Mandi? You don't owe him a thing." He searched my face for any sign of doubt, but found none. There was rage and hurt, but those would help me with what lay ahead.

"I'm sure." Mom stood a few feet away from Dad with a sad look on her face. My chest ached at her expression. "Mom." At the sound of my voice, her eyes met mine. "I love you."

"I love you, too." Her whispered and dejected words made my veins throb with the ire I held within me.

"We'll talk when I get back in, okay?" Nodding, she turned her attention to Hunter, but I cut her off before she could speak. "He won't be back." I left no room for argument before walking to the front door and opening it wide. "Let's go. I don't have all day."

I DIDN'T STOP UNTIL I REACHED HIS CAR AND LEANED AGAINST IT—there was no point in hiding my intentions. After our talk, he needed to leave. Hunter had caused me more problems in one day than I remember having in the last year.

"Say what you have to, and then leave." Hunter stopped beside me and mirrored my position. Together we watched the sun set, something that in the past we loved to do. Now his mere presence bothered me.

He took in a deep breath and groaned low. Almost too low for me to hear. "You still smell sweet, like the same lotion I used to buy you at the store inside of Sunset Place."

"I wore that scent before I met you. It's never changed." My voice was just as low as his. The anger had ebbed a bit, but what lingered now was mixed with what felt familiar. He was familiar to me.

We'd spent years together. Hunter was my first boyfriend. My first kiss. The first and only man to make love to me.

His shoulders sagged as he turned to face me. "I'm sorry, Mandi. So sorry."

Nodding, I acknowledged his apology but made no move to

verbally tell him he was forgiven. It was too soon, and one measly apology wasn't changing what he'd put me through.

After he left, I doubted myself. Why didn't he love me enough to work through the separation? Fuck that. I would've changed schools to be with him if he would've just asked.

Instead, he pushed me away. One day we were together and the next he was gone, and I was left crying over my first love. It had hurt. Still did in a sense.

"Why are you here, Hunter? Be honest with me. You left to study music and spread your wings. What happened?"

Hunter took a hold of my hand, and I let him. He squeezed it and pulled me to sit on the trunk of his car. Once situated, we leaned back and looked up at the sky. I sensed he was trying to gather his thoughts.

And I was trying not to think of Camden. Would he be infuriated with me if he knew I was with Hunter? Sitting close enough that our knees touched and talking about our past relationship?

"New York wasn't what I expected. Not one bit," Hunter began, bringing my attention to him. "I missed you the moment I got off the plane."

"Funny," I deadpanned, "because I didn't hear from you for almost six months to the date that you left."

He hopped off the trunk and paced in front of me. Agitated. "Would you have talked to me if I called? Be honest here."

"Yes." It wasn't a lie either. I waited for that phone call for weeks after he left.

"Fuck," Hunter shouted into the open night and came to stand before me. He reached out with the tips of his fingers to caress my face; I pulled back before he could. The act felt wrong. It wasn't his touch I wanted.

"Again, why are you here?" His hazel eyes met mine. They burned with fire and desire. I'd seen that look many times in the past. Where it once incensed my own need for his touch, I now felt cold.

"What's Camden to you? Are you just fucking him?"

How dare he? "Get the fuck off my property, Hunter. I don't want you here." He reached for me again, this time, his hands caging my face between them. "Get off."

"No. Not until you tell me the truth."

"Fuck you," I spat and pulled his hands away. With my knee, I pushed him and hopped off the car giving him my back. "You have no right to ask. Remember, it was you who left while I stayed here, waiting for you to tell me it was a mistake. That you loved me!"

"I still love you," he yelled back. "That was the biggest mistake of my life, Mandi. Young and dumb are the only way to describe my reasoning, but it's the God's honest truth. All I wanted was to just be me, without the *you* attached for once. We'd spent those last two years together, and I was selfishly thinking about having fun and seeing what college had to offer. I made a mistake. Why can't you accept that?"

I spun back around to face him, my eyes shooting daggers his way. "Goddamn selfish prick. You left me, so you could sleep your way through the NYU female student body. *Jesus*." There was no need to continue rehashing this shit. It wouldn't change my thoughts on him. He broke my heart for pure vain and selfish reasons.

"But I'm here now, Mandi. We loved each other." The nerve of this ass. He stopped my pacing, reaching out and pulling me to him by the elbow.

"Don't," I warned and pushed him away with the arm he wasn't holding. "Just don't."

"Mandi, can't you see I came back for you? For us?" With one strong pull, he had me in his arms. Our bodies were pressed together, his head coming toward me. Eyes focused on my lips. "I love you."

I slapped him before his lips touched mine. "But I don't love you." Hunter stood frozen; his arms loosened enough for me to escape his embrace. "Like I said inside, there's nothing for you here. Leave."

"Amanda," he called once more, but I ignored him and walked straight back into the house. I didn't wait for him to leave, didn't care if he spent the entire night outside. Hunter Knox was no longer my problem.

The house was quiet as I entered. All the lights, except for the one just inside the entrance, were off. It was just as well—I had nothing left in me today.

Between Hunter, my mother, and Camden; I was done.

TWELVE
Amanda

The house was empty by the time I made it downstairs the next morning. No note from either of them. Nothing.

At the very least, I was owed an apology, an honest conversation where she explained her erroneous logic and I made her see that what she did was wrong. How could Mom have been so stupid? In what universe was it okay to invite your daughter's ex-boyfriend to the house without informing her first?

The anger from last night had carried over, and I wanted to be anywhere but here. What a mess.

It didn't sit well with me to be angry with her. She'd always been a good mom—pushy, but good and supportive nonetheless. Could I fault her for wanting for me what she found in Dad? No, never, but trying to implement what she considered the right choice was just wrong.

Instead of dwelling, I decided to do as everyone else had done and avoid. They left, and frankly, so could I.

Grabbing my phone off the charger, I headed down and toward the kitchen. First on the agenda was coffee. There was what looked to be a fresh pot already made on the counter, my favorite princess mug placed beside it along with the sugar.

After pouring a cup, I took a seat at the counter and swiped my finger across my phone's screen. I needed my girls.

"Hey, Mandi. What's up?" Courtney answered on the second ring. It seemed to be windy wherever she was.

"Nothing much," I sighed and took a sip of the scalding liquid. It burned the tip of my tongue, but it would be worth the caffeinated boost of energy.

"What's wrong, babe? You sound like shit."

Felt like it too. "Rough twenty-four hours." Another sip of coffee. "Where are you?"

"I'm about to start buying the necessities for camp. Please tell me you're packed." I'd forgotten about this. Fuck.

Coach had set us up with a local athletic program for teens. We'd volunteered to spend time with them and help them work on their skills, whether it be shooting or improving their offense and defensive tactics.

"Fuck…shit…no."

She laughed at my response, and the wind level around her died down. "I'm at the Sports Authority in Kendall. Get dressed and head over here. We'll shop and grab some lunch afterward?"

"Sounds good." And it did. Being here felt awkward at the moment. "It'll take me an hour to get there, though."

"That's fine. I'm looking at sneakers now, and you know I take forever to pick a pair. Just head toward the shoe department when you come in. I'm sure I'll still be sitting here."

We hung up then, and I rushed up the stairs to get ready.

I stripped out of my pajamas as I made my way into the en suite bathroom. The tiled floor felt cold beneath my feet. Turning the water on, I waited for it to adjust before I entered. We might live in Florida, but freezing cold showers were never fun.

The bathroom quickly filled with steam and the mirrors grew foggy.

Reaching a hand in, I tested the water and stepped inside. A moan escaped the moment I stood underneath the shower-head. I'd been tense, and my muscles rejoiced in the pleasure the hot water afforded.

I didn't have much time to waste, so I reached and grabbed my mango passion body wash. Lathering myself, I encountered a new problem, though. The feel of the hot water and the washcloth across my skin felt good.

My nipples pebbled and throbbed as the suds slid down my chest and abdomen. It felt like the heated caress of the oil Camden used on me. Dropping the washcloth, I poured a small amount of the liquid soap in my hands and began to knead my breasts.

"Oh God," I whimpered as my fingers grazed over the hardened tips. My breathing became labored as I cupped them and squeezed, flushed with desire. I released one and skimmed a hand down my abs and over my mound.

His eyes were at the forefront of my thoughts as I grazed a finger over my engorged clit. It throbbed, and I bucked against my hand. In my head, it was his hands that touched me. They teased me to the point of having to hold onto the wall as I rubbed tight circles over my bundle of nerves.

"Goddamned sexy son of a bitch." I slammed my other hand against the glass tiles as ripples of pleasure coursed through me. My mind replayed the way he took control over me yesterday. My fingers mimicked the perfect spanks his cockhead gave me. "Conceited, gorgeous asshole. You're driving me insane, Camden."

One more spank, and I entered myself roughly with two fingers, the same way he'd slammed in almost twenty-four hours ago. Between the hot water grazing my flesh and the vision of his head thrown back—muscles strained as he entered me—I came.

My mouth opened in a silent scream. Everything felt more intense, heightened by the mere thought of him.

With my head against the wall, I tried to calm my breathing. Body weak and sated, I shook with the small aftershocks. How did a man I barely knew have this much power over me?

Hunter never made me feel this crazed. He never made me yearn to the point of madness for his cock. A cock I'd only felt once.

I was in more trouble than I'd originally thought.

"About time," Court complained as soon as she saw me. She was sitting on a small bench with more than ten shoe boxes around her. "You take the scenic route?"

"Where the hell is there a scenic route in the middle of Miami?" I'd underestimated the afternoon traffic while driving here. Bumper-to-bumper traffic sucked. "Can't decide?"

She shrugged and pulled out a pair of neon orange high-tops. "Too many to choose."

I made my way through the mountain beside her and took a seat at the edge of the bench. Court and I shared the same shoe size, and I needed a new pair of sneakers to take to camp. All the ones I had at home were too old—worn down to the point of almost falling apart.

"Here." She pushed a box into my hands. "I think you might like these."

Opening the box, I pulled out a pair of all black Nikes with a tri-color checkmark. They were perfect, and any other day, I would have squealed at the sight of them. Today wasn't one of those.

"They're cute," I added nonchalantly while I slipped one of the shoes on. They fit well and were comfortable. "I'm taking them, thanks."

"Okay. What the hell is going on with you?" She watched me, gaze boring a hole into my skull.

"Hunter." Her eyes narrowed as his name passed my lips. "He happened. Again."

Courtney took a hold of my hand and squeezed. "Fucking prick," she muttered low enough so only I heard. "Where did you see him?"

"At the spa, he cornered me—"

"Why would he be at the spa?" she interrupted.

A bitter laugh escaped me then. "Mom forgot to mention he works there now."

"Are you kidding me?"

I let out a frustrated sigh while staring at the active-wear across from us. "She also invited him to dinner without informing me. Let's just say that the entire night turned into a fight—I fought with him and *her*."

"Oh, Mandi." Courtney pulled me into a hug. A small tear escaped, and I tried to wipe it away before she'd notice. It didn't work. "Fuck this. Grab your shoes and let's go."

"Go? Go where?" Courtney ignored me; instead, she pulled me up and toward the cash register. "Court, wait."

"Yes?" She turned to look at me as we reached the counter. Her fingers had been flying over the screen of her phone. Looked like she was texting someone.

"Where are we going?" I placed my box next to hers on the counter. "What's the rush?"

"You still have your beach bag in the trunk?" She ignored my question and pushed my box with hers—swiping her card in the reader before I could complain. "You're buying dinner tonight."

"Sounds good."

"Now, answer. Do you have your bag?"

"You know I do." It'd been a habit I picked up from mom. Always carry extra clothes and a beach bag with everything you need just in case.

"Good, now hurry up. The girls are meeting us at the beach in an hour."

THE WAVES CRASHED UPON THE SHORE, LOW AND MAJESTIC IN THEIR unique color—the color of Camden's eyes. Looking out across the water was like drowning in them.

They pulled you in with their uniqueness. Engulfed, and lured you in without any intent to let you go.

"Are you going to stare out into space all day, or talk?" Jennifer called out, bringing my attention back to the present. She dug into the small cooler Steph brought and passed me a beer. "What did he do now?"

"He showed up." My eyes wandered back toward the water as I took a sip. "Showed up, claiming me in front of—"

"In front of who, Mandi?" Stephanie interrupted. Courtney and Jennifer leaned in closer; they shared the same look of curiosity. "You never mentioned seeing anyone."

Taking another sip, I turned to face them. If anyone could understand and not judge me, it would be these girls.

"It's new, and already ruined." I couldn't keep the sadness out of my tone. Between Hunter's bullshit and Camden being adamant that there would never be an "us", I was lost. "Where do you want me to begin?"

"What does that mean, babes? Ruined?" Courtney abandoned her chair across from me and sat by my feet. "You aren't making sense."

"Do you girls remember the night at Rage after winning the championship? The guy I danced with?" They nodded. "I've been seeing him. Well, not seeing per se…I'd say more like fooling around with."

"No shit!" Jennifer blurted out; choking on the sip she'd just taken from her bottle. "When?"

"The real question here is where?" Steph eyed me with sadness as she spoke.

I shook my head. "That's not the important part here, Steph. We bumped into each other, and he recognized me. We talked, things happened, and Hunter found me walking with him. Fuck. You should've heard the shit he spewed."

"I'm not surprised." Court shrugged apologetically. "He's always been an ass. Sorry, Mandi." I waved her off. It was the truth, and it took him leaving for me to see how one-sided our relationship had been. "Hunter's an insecure and possessive jerk who left you for purely selfish reasons."

"Let's just say that my friend didn't take it well. Words were exchanged, and then Hunter was knocked on his ass for being rude to me." Laughter bubbled out as I replayed the image in my head. "That part I enjoyed, and can you believe Hunter had the nerve to act offended when I told him to leave? In his head, he believes he still has a claim over me."

"And he doesn't?" Jennifer hedged softly.

"No." I'd never been more sure of my feelings than I was at that moment. There was nothing left in me for him. "But it didn't end there…oh, no. Then, he proceeded to inform me that Mom had invited him for dinner and to not be late."

"Jesus." Courtney shook her head and squeezed my hand.

"It was one clusterfuck after another. From our encounter, to my lunch with Cam—"

"Cam?" Steph interrupted again.

Picking the label off my bottle, I nodded. "Yeah, his name is Camden." Courtney smiled at me. She knew who he was, and by the look on her face, she'd put the pieces together. She now knew why every Wednesday for the last couple of weeks I'd been at the spa. "He's great, but it won't work between us."

"Why?" Jennifer jumped in, not missing a beat. My eyes wandered back over to the water, and I sighed. It reminded me of him, and his absence hurt. It shouldn't feel like this.

I didn't understand why it felt like this with him.

"Because all he wants is a fuck buddy, and that's not me. Do I like him? Yes, but eventually emotions will get involved, and I don't want to end up hurt."

"Then don't let them get involved. Walk away before they do." It was easier said than done, but I didn't say that to Steph.

"Over lunch yesterday, we argued, and I left him with an ultimatum of sorts. I told him he was on borrowed time." Taking in a deep breath, I let the smell of the sea fill my lungs. Once upon a time, that smell calmed me, but now it wrecked my fragile nerves. He smelled of the sun and waters that crashed upon the shore before me. "Then, I get home and Hunter's there, all smiles, sitting with Mom in the living room. There's no other way to explain what happened, but I exploded."

"You know I love your mom, Mandi, but she's out of line." Courtney pursed her lips in displeasure. "She ambushed you, and what? Expected that because he was there, and smiling, you'd fall into his arms?"

"Something like that."

"Fuck Hunter." Steph's voice held so much venom as she spat his name. "He walked away. Just left and didn't care. He doesn't deserve a single minute of your time. I say have fun with this Camden guy and let Hunter crawl back into the hole he came from."

"Amen." The other two agreed.

"What about Mom, though?"

"Susana loves you and worries. It's normal. Talk to her and explain how betrayed you felt and that she needs to respect your decisions enough to not interfere." Jennifer was right. Mom loved me. She wanted nothing but the best for me, but her idea of what I needed and mine were very different.

"Okay." Court stood and dusted the sand off her ass. "Enough with the heavy shit—let's get in the water and enjoy this beautiful day."

Laughing, I pushed her back on her ass and ran toward the water. Enough was enough, and they were right. Hunter walked away, and I no longer loved him. He didn't matter.

Talking to them helped. Made me rationalize things that last night seemed like a lost cause, that overwhelmed me. Not one of them involved my ex.

They all surrounded the man with beautiful eyes and strong hands that had turned my quiet life on its axis. A man that no matter how much I knew would hurt me, I couldn't walk away from.

THIRTEEN

Amanda

"Jesus." I groaned in pain. We'd been at camp for the last few days and I wanted to die. The kids were brutal—a good kind of brutal—and my body was protesting. Laughter exploded next to me, and I rolled my eyes. "Shut it, Matt."

Matt was a counselor here, only two years older than me and cute. He'd become good friends with the girls and me. Didn't hurt that he was also very gay and completely at ease with all the bull crap we gossiped about.

He'd been a distraction. Fun. Matt doesn't let me dwell on my problems at home or the many phone calls from Hunter and Camden I'd ignored.

"Get up, champ," he snickered and pulled me to my feet. I'd been laying on the grassy area next to the basketball court for the last ten minutes trying to rest up. The kids had been called in for lunch, and I was still trying to regulate my breathing. "How is it that the state champion is already sore? You should be used to this much physical activity."

My first instinct was to flip him off, but I couldn't. Not while at the camp site, at least. Instead, I maturely stuck my tongue out and crawled over to my gym bag by the makeshift bleachers. Opening the bag, I pulled out a bottle of water and took a few sips.

The heat index was above a hundred today, and I was feeling every scorching degree.

"It's not that I'm tired." Matt rolled his eyes at my obvious lie. I'd done nothing but whine since they left to eat. "Fine. I'm exhausted. Not even our coach's most rigorous drill could have prepared me for those tween overachievers. They were amazing, but damn, they didn't give me a second to catch my breath."

Matt nodded and took a seat beside me on the bench. "This group is hungry to learn. Excited. Can you blame them, though? You have to remember what it was like to be that age and competitive."

With a smile on my face, I bumped his shoulder. "I do. Probably was a lot worse, too."

"You're horrible now," he laughed. "The way you coach and work them through the drills, I would've hit you with a basketball already. Right to the back of the head when you weren't looking."

"Ass," I muttered low and raised my head to hit him when my phone rang, pulling my attention toward my gym bag.

"But you love me," Matt sang, and I laughed. The man could be such a dork at times.

The phone stopped ringing, only to begin again a few seconds later. There was only one way to explain why I picked up the call, and it could only be described as instinctual. It was second nature to grab the small device and swipe my finger over its screen.

I was an idiot.

"Hello," the voice on the other end yelled, and I flinched. Camden sounded angry. "Amanda, where the hell are you? It's already ten past three."

"Answer, woman," Matt urged, and it was a huge mistake. I knew the moment the innocent words passed through his lips that this would blow up into something unnecessary.

"Cam—"

"Who the fuck is that?" Camden interrupted, his anger barely contained. He had a lot of nerve.

My mind told me to hang up, that he didn't have the right to question me. We were nothing.

But my heart, that idiotic muscle, pumped furiously at the mere sound of his voice.

My skin flushed, and it wasn't the sun's punishing beams that caused the pink hue. It was him. The memory of what occurred just last week.

"Hello, Camden. How are you?" Matt raised an eyebrow at my nonchalant response, but I ignored him. It was beyond me how I managed to speak with the sudden dryness in my mouth.

The images of us last week hit me all at once.

How commanding he was, the way he tugged furiously on his cock as he watched my fingers disappear between my soaked lips during our last session.

"I asked a question, *gatita.*" He snarled, his anger scorching me through the phone. "Who the fuck was that?" A shiver ran through me, and Matt's eyes widened as he realized what this man's mere voice did to me.

If it weren't for the fucked up situation I was now caught in, even I'd laughed at my bumbling behavior.

"I'm going to…" Matt pointed toward the campsite's mess hall. "Yeah, I'll catch you later, Mandi."

Nodding, I turned to face the empty basketball court. "Watch the tone, Camden. I don't owe you an explanation. We're nothing, remember? Just two people that hooked up. No strings."

There was a sudden loud crash that made me gasp, like glass meeting a hard surface and shattering. My absence couldn't have affected him that much. I didn't matter to him.

"What do you want?" I asked, deflated, tired in every sense of the word.

"You, *here* with me." The frustrated sigh that escaped him didn't evade my notice. I could almost see him pacing the floor of his massage room, jaw set in a hard line.

"I'm getting tired of you pulling me in with one hand, only to push me away with the other." My legs felt weak, unsteady as I sat down again on the bench. "You can't have it both ways."

"Tell me something I don't know, *gatita.* I'm tired of wanting you so much—I can't look at another woman without feeling guilt. Misplaced guilt, because last I checked, I belong to no fucking one."

Jesus. Those words hurt. "When have I asked you to belong to me?" There was a basketball on the floor next to the bench I was sitting on. Before I could stop myself, I kicked it with all my might. The ball flew across the court and into a small bush on the other side. It was either that, or punch the wooden bench, and I couldn't afford to hurt my hand. "You're the one calling, getting jealous and demanding answers to questions you have no right to ask."

"Amanda, I…fuck." His breathing was harsh and angry. "Look, *gatita*, I don't want to fight. All I wanted to know is where you were. Why you aren't here?"

Grabbing a small hand towel from my bag, I wiped my face down and took in a deep breath. "I'm at a summer camp for teenage athletes. It's a county-wide program for these kids, and I participate every year, along with the girls from my team."

"Team?" Camden asked.

"Yes, team." How did he not know this? "I play for the University of Miami's women's basketball team."

"Really? What position?"

Did he think I was bullshitting him? "Point guard," I huffed while looking up toward the heavens. The clouds were coming out, and the sky had started to darken. "I've played since the age of ten. It's my dream to play in the WNBA."

"But you're so tiny." There was a small tinge of awe in his voice.

"I'm five-six, you ass. Not tiny at all. I'm average height, but deadly on the court. There's a reason why we're state champions."

"Holy shit," Camden breathed out. "You're serious?"

"Like a heart attack." The sky opened up then, the rain coming down on me in a light sprinkling. His breathing on the other end had calmed down some. Slowed. "Listen, Cam—"

"When can I see you?" It wasn't a request. More like a command disguised as one.

"Don't know," I breathed out slow. I'd already begun walking toward the nearest cabin. "We're scheduled to be here for the rest of the week. I'll call you."

"Are you in town?" Camden pushed. It felt good to know he missed me. At the least, he missed my body and the wetness that pooled between my thighs for him.

"I am, but I'll be busy until next week." A small pang of hurt fluttered through my chest. It sucked. As much as I hated admitting this, I missed him. Missed the way he made me feel when I was within his arms. His touch. "Promise I'll call you when I get back home."

"Not good enough. I need to see you, *gatita*." It was the first time I'd heard him be so open. Vulnerable. "Please."

"Don't put me on the spot like this." The rain had picked up, as the heavens opened and poured down around me. "I miss you."

His sharp intake of breath let me know he'd heard. "Miss you, too." It was said low, almost too low for me to hear.

"Good." *Really…good?*

"Good," he mimicked with a bit of mirth. "How about you have fun doing this camp thing and call me the second you get home?"

"Maybe." I threw my head back and laughed. The conversation had taken on a much lighter tone. "You'll just have to wait and see."

"Or I can always come looking for you. See who was—"

"Camden," I interrupted.

"Yeah?"

"I'll see you next week. And by the way…"

"What?"

"He's gay." Swiping my finger across the screen, I disconnected the call before he could utter another word. My phone rang two seconds after I'd hung up. His name flashed across the screen, I hit ignore and made a mad dash across the wet pavement toward the counselor's lounge.

With this weather, it was obvious that the afternoon's activities were canceled for the day. *Maybe I'd be lucky and catch a nap.*

I doubted it, and the looks my girls were giving me as I entered only confirmed this. As I took a seat next to Courtney, I knew one thing for certain: there would be no sleeping in my near future.

"Spill," Courtney said, confirming my suspicions. This was going to be a long day.

"I'M HOME," I YELLED INTO THE EMPTY KITCHEN, DROPPING MY BAG next to the door. They were home; I'd seen both of their cars parked inside our spacious garage. "Where is everyone?"

"In the living room." Dad's deep baritone voice carried over from the other side of the house. The last time I'd come home, and they were in the living room, things hadn't ended well. That fight still hadn't been discussed. Avoidance had been key by both parties involved.

"How was camp, sweetheart?" Mom looked up from her magazine long enough to ask. She seemed hesitant still.

"Mom," I said with my eyes firmly set on hers. "I'm sorry."

She was out of her seat and hugging me before I finished my sentence. "No, Mandi. I'm sorry…so sorry. I just thought you'd be happy," she cried, her tears falling onto my thin tank top. "I thought you still loved him."

Shaking my head, I pulled back enough for her to see my face. "Not anymore. The Hunter you know, and the one I dated, are two very different people. He's a jerk, and I never want to see him again."

Mom swiped her fingers under my eyes, catching the stray tears that fell. "What did he do?"

"Did he ever explain to you why he left?"

She shook her head. "No."

"Then sit down. I think it's time you find out the real reason why he threw me away." Looking toward the chair Dad had occupied, I found it empty. It was better this way. There were just some things no father needed to hear.

Especially if they were as overprotective as mine tended to be.

Mom sat down on the love seat and pulled me down next to her. With my hand in hers, she spoke. "Please, tell me."

"There isn't a simple way for me to say this, so here goes." I took in a deep breath then and told her everything. Why he left, and why I wasn't enough—the fight outside last week and what he wanted from me.

"I'm sorry, baby," Mom croaked beside me. "I didn't know."

"It's okay." Wrapping my arm around her shoulder, I pulled her close and gave her a squeeze before wiping away the few tears that had fallen. "Look, I know you meant well, but next time…talk to me. Don't assume, okay?"

She nodded and kissed my cheek. "Understood." Mom watched me with a small smile on her face. "Enough of the bad. Let's talk about the new guy Hunter mentioned. Do we know him?"

"You do. In fact, I met him because of your pushing." Her brows furrowed in confusion before they arched in understanding. My own smile grew.

"Oh, fuck," Mom cursed, and I couldn't contain my giggle. The prim and proper Susana Brooks dropping an F-bomb in casual conversation. Priceless. "Camden?"

"Yeah," I said laughing, "but it's new. Nothing serious. Just two people getting to know the other with no strings attached. Taking it slow." *At an almost nonexistent pace*, I added mentally. "He's sweet and—"

"Old," Mom pointed out. "He's at the very least ten years your senior baby. What could you possibly have in common?"

Oh, nothing. Except, my need for his cock and the fact that my pussy wants it above all others.

"Camden's age means nothing to me." Her brow rose skeptically, and my eyes narrowed. This was why I hadn't felt the need to share. "We like each other. He makes me laugh and happy, and that should be more than enough for you to drop the age gap crap. Especially, with Dad being almost twelve years *your* senior."

"Amanda, it's not the same, and you know it. Things were different when I—"

"Save it, Mom," I hissed out and stood up to leave. Why did she always have to add in her two cents? For once, I'd like her to just trust my judgment. "I'm not asking for permission here. Just sharing with whom my interest lay. It will never be Hunter and me. Never."

"Agreed," Mom said through pursed lips. "Hunter doesn't deserve you, but Camden is a man, sweetheart, and I don't think you're ready for a relationship like that."

Bending at the waist, I laid a kiss on her forehead and walked away. I stopped as my right foot landed on the first step and turned to face her.

"Thank you for the vote of confidence, Mom, but luckily, what you think doesn't matter. Not your choice to make. If I do or don't, it will be my decision." With that, I left her and carried my tired butt upstairs. It's not that I wanted to be rude or hurt her feelings, but on this, I wouldn't budge.

This man had managed to burrow himself under my skin, and I didn't want him to leave. There was something between us that grew with each interaction we had, and I wanted to explore that "what if."

With my mind made up, I pulled out my phone from my back pocket and shot off a quick text to him.

Meet me in an hour at Bayside. ~gatita

FOURTEEN
Amanda

"Going somewhere?" Mom asked as we passed each other in the hall. It was Wednesday, and I was on my way to see Camden. We haven't seen each other in two weeks, and my need for him was almost to the point of pain.

When I'd messaged him a few days back, he was already out with friends, watching a ball game and having a few beers. He wanted to see me but had already made plans, and I wasn't the clingy type to demand he come to me.

I almost wished that I was that kind of woman. The type that wouldn't take no for an answer because I yearned for his hands over my skin. For the way he pushed his fingers—maneuvered my body to his liking.

"What gave you that idea?" My reply had a bit of a bite to it. Mom had made her displeasure on the subject known; she didn't trust me enough to handle a relationship with a man like Camden. Thought I was too naïve.

She eyed the simple white romper I wore and smiled. "Heading to the beach with the girls today? That's good; maybe they can talk some sense into you."

"No, I'm not." Her smile turned quickly into a frown. Looking down at the short, white linen outfit I wore, I didn't see what made her think I was heading to the beach. Yes, it was simple, but it was also tight and molded onto the flesh of my ass in a borderline indecent way. The top portion was strapless and tied in the center with a cute bow; it drew the eyes to my breasts without showing much skin.

Provocative, yet demure—innocent yet not—it was perfect for me to seduce Camden with, and push him into devouring me. Give me what I needed.

"Then where are you going?" I'd almost forgotten that she was here as my mind wandered to the endless possibilities this afternoon would bring.

"Since when do you need to know my every movement? I'm not a child, Mother—"

"I know you're not." She sighed and gave me a small smile. "Please, just be careful, Mandi. I'll butt out and keep my opinions to myself, but if you get hurt…"

Mom meant well, I knew this, but she needed to realize that nothing short of Camden telling me to fuck off would make me give him up.

Nodding, I leaned in and kissed her cheek before heading straight to the garage and my car. The drive over to the hotel this time was filled with delicious anxiety. Fluttering wings of anticipation took over my stomach, and the smile on my face never vanished.

You love him.

No, that couldn't be it. Could it?

We didn't know each other—interact enough—for me to feel this way. It took me almost a year to say I love you to Hunter, and even that was because he pushed and pushed until I said it back. Did I come to love him? Yes, I did, with everything that I was at that stage in my life.

It was sweet and new—young and unmarred by life's unrelenting evils.

Valet parking was empty as I pulled in; the same kid from the previous times came towards me with a smile on his face. He noticed my grimace the closer he got and threw his hands up in the air.

"I swear on all that's holy that nothing will happen to this beauty," he exclaimed, and I couldn't stop the laughter that erupted from within me. Little shit seemed all too proud of how he'd recognized my fear and tried to assuage it. "If it happens, any damage sustained," he spoke as if reading a manual, "I'll pay for. Or my mom will, but she might kill me, so I'll be extra careful."

After stepping out of my car, I tossed him the keys, still giggling at his antics. "Okay. I'll trust you, but one scratch and…" I trailed off, and he gulped. I walked toward the door of the hotel, my heart thundering in my chest with each step I took.

The palms of my hands began to sweat the moment the spa's name—with its bold letters—came into view. However, none of that mattered the moment my eyes landed on him standing outside. The same spot we'd met at the last time I was here.

His lips curved into a wicked grin, and I bit mine. It was only when we were face to face that my body succumbed to the exhaustion of these last few days.

I'd pushed myself beyond my limit with all the drills we performed this last week. I gave the same intensity with the kids, as I did, when we decided to play some of the other athletes at the camp. My body was sore, and it begged me to stay in bed today, but I needed to see him.

"What hurts, *gatita*?" He noticed right away and grasped my hand in his, pulling me to stand in front of him, close enough that I felt his body heat. Camden took in a deep breath once we stood less than a few inches apart; he inhaled in deeply and groaned. "Fuck, I've missed you."

Those words were what I needed above all else. They gave me comfort in pursuing him—breaking down his walls until he let me in.

"Missed you." I breathed in, and it was my turn to drown in his scent; a masculine smell so uniquely his that it drove me insane. "The last time we—"

"Shhh," Camden put his finger over my lips. "Not out here. Follow me." Before he pulled his finger away, I swiped the very tip with my tongue, just a small taste to hold me over until I had him alone and naked.

If there was one thing I wanted to get out of today's session, it was leaving the room with his taste still on my tongue. I wanted to feel the weight of him—feel his girth stretching my lips to accommodate his size.

"Follow me." Camden tapped my lips once in reproach before turning to walk back into the spa. He turned to face me before we passed the reception area. Blondie sat behind the desk, and she watched his every move with unrestrained hunger. "Sit, *gatita*," he whispered low enough so only I heard. "I'll be back in two."

"Cam," she called out before he could disappear. I didn't like the way she said his name. It held too much familiarity, as if they knew each other outside of business hours. "Can I speak to you about our plans this weekend?"

My eyes snapped up at the mention of plans. What the fuck?

Camden hadn't turned back to face her. He'd stopped walking, but other than that, he remained quiet. On the other hand, he hadn't denied it either.

She looked at me with a smug expression adorning her face, triumphant in her quest to agitate me. It was one of those moments where I truly felt I had no hold over him. None, yet he controlled me with just a single touch from his teasing hands.

"Quit it," Camden hissed out, bringing me back to the present. Her eyes and mine snapped toward his, his back still turned to the room. We had no clue if he was directing himself at her or me. "We have no plans, Cynthia."

"Yes, we do," Cynthia insisted in an embarrassing whimper. "The company's employee…" I tuned her out after that. Stupid bitch.

"Fucking quit it. There is no *we*. No plans either," he spit out in anger, and it aroused me. How easily he shut her down caused my panties to dampen and my inner thighs to glisten. "You're embarrassing yourself." Without sparing her another word, he turned his neck, met my eyes, and smirked. "I'll be right back, Amanda."

Nodding, I stayed put and waited. Cynthia didn't take long to strike. His footsteps had barely silenced when she opened her mouth to spew venom.

"You are nothing to him, but easy pussy. Not a fucking thing. Enjoy it while you can." Her words were meant to hurt, and had this conversation happened a year ago, I might have believed her. Now, though, her words meant shit.

"Who says I want more than his cock?" Her mouth dropped open, and she stared at me, wide-eyed, no longer cocky, and sure of herself. "Maybe all I'm after is a good fuck." A couple entered the reception area seconds after the word, "fuck" passed my lips. They smiled at me as I took a seat on the plush sofa and then they turned to ask for Hunter.

Cynthia continued to stare at me; a mixture of anger and resentment overtaking her expression. She wanted to say something, I could see it clear as day, but she couldn't. Too many people in the lobby to witness her unprofessionalism.

"Is she okay?" the woman who had taken a seat beside me asked, and I wanted to laugh. No, she wasn't okay. Her bullshit plan to hurt me had backfired, and she'd felt the sting of my bite.

I laughed and turned to address her. "She'll be fine. Just stunned by the story I shared with her. Right, Cynthia?" My tone was saccharine sweet and dripping with innocence.

She snapped back to the present at the mention of her name and nodded, turning to face the couple and ignoring me. Just as well, because I didn't give a flying fuck about her either.

"UNDRESS FOR ME."

Same words uttered as every other time, yet they sounded

different today. Soft. Not a command, but a desperate plea on his behalf to my body. He needed me to give myself to him, and I would.

Of that, there was never a doubt.

I walked a few paces ahead, just enough to create the space for me to disrobe. To tempt him with my naked flesh and the small white lace thong I wore beneath my romper.

A gasp left me at the sight of him watching me with hooded eyes. Camden stood in all his male glory before me, with no shirt on and a pair of thin white linen pants. I'd come to appreciate the way he posed in front of the door with each session. He leaned back against the room's only exit, arms crossed over his naked, broad chest as he waited for me to comply with his demands.

Pulling the small bow that sat at the center of my chest, I loosened the top enough to let it fall to my waist. My breasts were bared to him. His eyes raged—the blue and greens mixed into a frenzied storm of lust. They swept from peak to peak, making them stiff and throb with want.

"Come closer." The soft tone from a few minutes ago was gone. This was more like the man I knew. Shaking my head, I pushed down the rest of my clothes and let them pool at my feet. "Get the fuck over here."

"No."

Camden growled at my defiance, his fists clenched at his sides. "*Gatita*, I'm not in the mood for games. Come to me." Still, I defied him and instead took a seat at the very edge of his table.

"I need your hands, Camden." It was my turn to plead. His lip curled up, that gorgeous grin he wore during my first massage overtaking his face. It was sexy. Disarming. "Please."

"You do realize what you're asking for, right?"

"I do." And I did. He couldn't give me more now, but he would eventually. This man couldn't deny the flames that burned between us. It was more than a simple spark.

"Are you—"

"Please love me as only you can. Fuck me like no other has

before." My words—the truth behind them—pushed him off that door and over to me. He placed his hands on either side of my body on the narrow bed. Caged me in.

"There will be no other. Ever." Camden ran his nose down the side of my face, from my hair line to jaw. He nipped the skin there before running his tongue over the tender bite. "I won't allow it."

"Please," I begged again, arching into him. My thighs spread, accommodating his narrow waist, and allowed me to press my aching core against him. "Make the hurt go away."

"Hurt?" He pulled back and eyed me. His cock never quit flexing against the scrap of lace I still wore. Thick and heavy against my wet lips, it rubbed me. Felt so good.

"No." My whimper let him see, see the pain that not having him close had inflicted. "My pussy aches for you, baby."

"Is that so?" The cocky son of a bitch smirked at me and leaned in for a kiss. Turning my face at the very last second, he missed my lips and kissed my neck instead, right below my ear. A shiver ran through me at the contact.

I didn't answer; instead, I wrapped my legs around his waist and pulled him closer. His fingers tangled in my hair and turned my face toward his. Our eyes met. Intense desire reflected in his orbs, and I drowned in them.

"Fucking take what's yours," I choked out and made a move to lie back. Camden released my tresses, but not before stealing a quick sweet kiss from me, a total contradiction to the way he ground his cock against my wet pussy.

FIFTEEN

Amanda

I lay there on that massage table for him, open to his every whim, and all that I begged for in exchange was for him to touch me. To take and break what I so willingly gave. Camden eyed me with undisguised hunger while his fingers trailed up my leg.

"Baby, please." Goosebumps rose on my skin and a small whimper escaped my lips. My hips rose off the small table and undulated—seeking out his fingers.

"Don't fucking move." His hands spread out and his fingers dug into my fevered flesh. "We are doing this my way. Do you understand me, *gatita*? My fucking way."

"Anything you want. Just let me taste you." The neediness in my tone caused a loud growl to ripple from his chest. His fingers—the ones holding my thighs tightly in his grasp—pulled me down to the edge of the table and spun me around. Camden angled the bed a bit, pulling a lever beneath the table and lowering my head.

I now lay right below the bulge in his pants.

I could almost taste him. The white linen pants he wore hid nothing and I took advantage of it. Rising, I nuzzled him and licked the outline of his hard cock. His grunt was all the approval I needed, and before he could utter another word, I pulled the strings of his indecent pants and took out his dick.

It sprung out and smacked his lower abdomen, leaving a small bead of liquid over his hard muscles. My mouth watered at the sight. With one hand I pumped his cock, while my thumb swiped over the slit at the top and collected the moisture there.

"Goddamn frustrating woman," Camden hissed out while thrusting into my hand. My fist tightened around him, and his head fell back. The muscles in his stomach clenched with each swipe of my finger over his engorged head.

"Told you I wanted a taste." His head snapped back up, and his eyes darkened as he watched me bring the glistening digit to my lips. "Fuck, so good."

"Open," he demanded and pushed my hand away. He tapped the head of his cock against my lips, smearing his pre-come along them.

I opened my mouth and licked them—at once, his taste exploded on my tongue, and I moaned.

My thighs closed, and I rubbed them together. Wetness seeped out of my useless panties; they concealed nothing. The more I moved, the more exposed I became.

Flushed and panting, I looked up and into his lust-filled eyes. "More," I cried and pushed up to take the swollen tip into my mouth. Camden pulled back just a second before I did. "What the hell?"

"Move closer," he bit out and grasped my shoulders in his strong hands. The words had barely registered when he'd dragged my head over the edge of the table, the perfect height for him to fuck my mouth. Head hanging over the edge and lips parted, he would slide in without difficulty. "Much better, *gatita*. Don't you agree?"

"Yes."

Camden leaned over my body and ran his hand from the center of my chest to my pussy. His finger slid under the lace edge of my thong with each pass. Fingers spread and palm pressing down firmly, he massaged his way across my body until he cupped me firmly.

My wetness coating his fingers could be heard in the silence of the room.

"This responsive little pussy is mine." With his wet fingers, he parted my lips and played just outside my entrance. Not entering, just teasing me with slight pressure—light taps against the swollen lips. I squirmed beneath him. Between his touches and the weight of his hardness against my face, I was a wanton mess of heat.

"I want your cock in my mouth," I cried out as he circled a single finger over my clit. My hips rose off the table, but he simply pushed me down with the same hand coated in my wetness.

"Open," Camden ordered, and I complied. He placed the tip just outside my parted lips; his hand was back over my heated core, and as he pushed forward to enter my mouth, he fucked me with two fingers. "Fuck. So wet…hot."

"Oh God," I groaned around his dick before he pulled out again.

"This is what you wanted, to feel me hot and heavy against your tongue?" With my eyes set on his, I nodded and raised my head to take him in deeper. "Shit." His fingers stopped moving while he watched me take him down my throat. He was big, and I choked.

The hand on my pussy squeezed hard at the feel of my throat constricting around his girth. Camden released his hold on me and slid his fingers up my body until reaching my throat. Tenderly, he caressed my neck and the imprint of his cock inside.

"Love the way you look with my dick in your mouth," he grunted, pushing into my mouth at a slower pace now. No rush; he seemed to want to savor the feel of my lips wrapped around him. "It's almost obscene. So fucking dirty."

Pulling back a bit, I let him pop out of my mouth and dragged my tongue down toward his heavy balls. "You taste so good," I said before pulling one into my mouth and swirling my tongue around it while pumping his shaft with one hand.

"Motherfuck." His body trembled, and his cock swelled in my hand. "Enough." He growled, and I stopped; eyes wide and shivering at the anger in his tone. "When I come, it will be in your pussy. Not your hand or mouth."

I was his rag-doll. Camden manipulated my body in ways that Hunter had never achieved. He'd turned me to his liking with my ass now hanging off the edge of his table. How I didn't fall as he spun me around, I'd never know.

"Spread those beautiful legs, *gatita*." I automatically complied with his demand, spreading my legs as wide as the small table permitted. "Goddamned beautiful little pussy," he snarled before bending down and nuzzling me. His nose rubbed my clit, then he kissed my lips.

"Quit teasing me!" My scream of frustration caused him to let out a low chuckle. He sucked my lips into his mouth and let them slide out in slow motion.

"So good. So sweet." He breathed me in before standing back up to his full height. "But now, I want to see just how good you'll feel wrapped around my cock." With that, he grabbed his dick and rubbed the head along my wet slit. I could hear my wetness coat him, feel the way he trembled when his tip pressed against my heat.

"Please, I need—" The words caught in my throat as he pushed in. There was no way to describe the way he felt inside me. How he stretched me, a delicious burn that only intensified my hunger for this man.

It would only ever be for him.

"How…*fuck*." His hips met mine as his wild eyes looked down at me in wonder. "Why do you render me useless? How am I supposed to not get addicted to the feel of you, *gatita*?"

"Don't fight it." My hips lifted on their own accord, meeting his thrust. It was slow. Sensual. I pulled him down over me; my soul needed this closeness, and my body needed to feel his weight on me.

"Don't think I can." His face contorted in the perfect picture of painful bliss. A bead of sweat rolled down the side of his face and over his jaw. Reaching up, I sucked the skin between my teeth and whimpered. Everything of his tasted good. "Fuck." He pushed in harder. Deeper. My body trembled, and he let out a deep groan.

Camden's movements were worshipping. He pushed in hard—

the ridges of his cock dragged along the walls of my pussy. The head rubbed against my weakest point with each inward stroke, and I squeezed down on him.

His head rested on my shoulder, his arms wrapped around my upper back. Those hands—those long, glorious fingers were etching themselves into my shoulders. With each entry, he pulled me down to meet his thrust. Pain never felt so good.

"Harder. Please, I need you harder," I mewled low, my lips next to his ear.

Lifting his head, he looked down at me and shook his head. "Just feel me, *gatita*. Just feel." His pace slowed even more, small thrusts that drove me wild as he'd push in to the hilt and gyrated, his pelvis rubbing me where I throbbed the most. I felt every twitch, every inch of him. "Fuck, baby," he grunted with a sharper flex of his hips. "Squeeze me. Yeah, just like that…pussy so good."

"Oh God," I moaned low and kissed his sweet lips. They tasted of me. My essence on him only added to the fuel of desire that scorched my veins. At the feel of my tongue licking at his mouth, his hands left their perch on my shoulders and grasped onto my hips. He anchored me to the massage bed, held me down, and began to fuck me in earnest.

The sound of skin slapping was the only thing heard in the room. It was obscene; I could hardly breathe.

"Touch yourself." Camden's voice was like dousing my flame with kerosene. With my eyes set on his, I grabbed my breasts and squeezed them. My nipples pebbled, elongating into stiff peaks. He licked his lips while I pulled on them. His hips punished my teasing with hard strokes.

Crazed. Delirious. My hunger for him only grew.

I released one of my breasts, brought my fingers to his lips, and pushed them in. Camden sucked and swirled his tongue around them before I pulled them out. Wet and glistening, I brought them down across my stomach and over my clit. It was his spit and my juices combined that I used to get me off.

The crazed snarl that passed through his swollen lips made me gush. Drenched us both.

"Shit!" I yelled out as he pulled my legs up and over his elbows, spreading me wider. He looked down at me with a smirk on his face, challenging me to complain.

"Too much?" Camden taunted—cocky asshole that he is—slamming into me as my mouth opened to answer. I choked on my reply and rubbed my clit harder. There was no denying that I was almost there, all I needed was a little more.

"Motherfuck," I gasped. He'd pulled out and pushed my hand aside with his cock. Swollen and red, the tip rubbed me harshly as the rest of him slid through my bare lips. My body shook and thrashed on the tiny bed while he brought me over the edge. "Come on me, baby. Please, come on me."

"Son of a bitch," Camden roared as the first stream of come left him. It landed on my lower abdomen, he wasn't happy about that and stood over me. Cock in hand; he tugged harshly until all he had to give covered my abused pussy. "How is it that…" he took in a ragged breath "…that I just came, and I want to fuck you again. Now."

A tiny giggle escaped me. "Next time, I want to be on top."

"Agreed." He leaned over, not giving a fuck that our combined juices still covered me, and nipped my lower lip. "Let's get cleaned up and out of here."

"What about work?"

"You were my last appointment of the day." My smile widened at his words. "I thought it'd be nice if we went back to my place and made dinner. Maybe even watch a movie?"

"This sounds a lot like a date." He had to have heard the hope in my voice. Maybe this was his way of saying he also wanted more.

"It does," was his reply before walking over to the small table beside the bed and grabbing a towel. Camden was gentle while cleaning me. Reverent. The entire act was worth more to me than everything we'd done so far.

After he'd cleaned us up, we both got dressed and headed out the door. Not hand in hand, but close enough that I felt the heat of his body on my back. He was only a step behind me, hardly any separation between our sated bodies as we walked into the main reception area.

We were a few feet away from the door when Hunter walked in, a scowl on his face as he took in our nearness. He made a move to come closer and then stopped, his eyes trained on Camden. "I'm not giving up on her, asshole. She was once mine and will be again."

Hunter's statement only caused the man behind me to let out a deep and loud laugh. "The operative word in the garbage you just spewed was *'once.'* Past tense, motherfucker. Now," Camden said, pulling my back against his hard chest, "she belongs to me. Fuck with mine again and—"

"And what?" Hunter pushed, chest puffed out in a total show of his masculinity. In my opinion, he looked stupid. The entire conversation was ridiculous.

Camden chuckled before kissing the side of my neck. "Simple. I'll tell her why you're *really* back. What you told my family, so they'd hire your pathetic ass."

I gasped and turned to look at Camden. "What does that mean?"

"Nothing," Hunter hissed, his cold eyes trained on the man beside me. "It means nothing."

"Like he said, *gatita*." Camden winked and pushed me forward. "It means nothing."

As pissed as being in the dark made me, whenever he used that name, I couldn't stop smiling.

We passed an irate Hunter on the way out the main door. They were both quiet as we passed, and I was left stewing in my own thoughts. I'd be damned if they kept me in the dark.

I'd use whatever I had at my disposal to get the information out of Camden. My pussy was in for a long night.

SIXTEEN
Amanda

"How I've never run into you before blows my mind." I shook my head. Camden raised a brow as we walked into the private elevator to his condo. "I've been in this high-rise quite a few times."

His lips formed a thin line. "Who do you know that lives here?"

"A friend." I rolled my eyes at his impatient huff. Pushing off the wall, I came to stand in front of him and fisted his shirt. He smirked at my actions, but let me pull him down to my level nonetheless. "I have many friends, you know."

"As long as they have pussies—"

I bit his lip, cutting him off mid-sentence. "I'll have you know, that a woman or two have hit on me in the past. Gender doesn't matter in that aspect."

"And have you?" His arms wound around my waist, pulling me in just a tiny bit closer. I could feel his hardness against my stomach. "Let a woman taste what doesn't belong to you?" With his fingers tangled in the ends of my hair, he tilted my head back and kissed the hollow of my throat. "Answer me."

"That isn't any of your business." Camden bit me in response, and I let out a small hiss. "I'm not asking you details about your past…am I?"

"Fair enough, but I still want to know who you came to see."

"A girl from the team—our captain—used to live here before graduating and moving to Boston for a job." Another kiss. "We spent a few days here over the summer, going to the beach and tanning. Using the gym and flirting with a few of the other cute male tenants." His eyes narrowed, and his grip on my hair tightened. "But don't worry, nothing happened. I've been with no one since—" I stopped right there, knowing he'd know who I was referring to anyway.

"For some reason, that doesn't make me feel any better."

"It wasn't meant to." The elevator reached his floor then. The doors opened; he pulled me behind him and into a very spacious and open living room.

"Do you want the tour now or after dinner?" For the first time since I'd met Camden, he looked nervous. Out of place.

"You were serious about dinner?" He nodded and then did the cutest thing. Camden blushed. It broke me to see him so shy all of a sudden, and now this date meant so much more than what I'd had in mind. To me, this was his way of proving I was more than just a convenient lay to him.

"We can order out? Something simple."

"No." Fine, we'd do this his way.

"Then what are we cooking?" I still had no idea if the man knew his way around the kitchen, and I didn't feel like playing the guinea pig.

"How do you feel about us grilling outside? I make a mean stuffed lamb burger." My stomach rumbled then, and it was my turn to blush. "Guess that's a yes."

Nodding, I let him pull me through the living area and into a very well-stocked kitchen. "I'm impressed," I said and smacked his ass as he opened the fridge and pulled out an already thawed pack of what I assumed was ground lamb. "What can I do to help?"

From what I could see, he had all the ingredients I'd need for my mom's potato salad. It wouldn't take me long at all to prepare and would go great with the burgers.

"How about for sides? Got any ideas?" Camden walked over to the sliding glass doors and opened them. Immediately, the smell of the water below hit me, and I inhaled deep. "Why are you smiling?"

"I love that smell." He nodded, but didn't ask for more of an explanation. With his hands full of ingredients, he set up a workstation on the counter space beside me. I watched him as he created a kind of chimichurri for the lamb. Sexiest thing I've ever seen—Camden in all his masculine glory doing something so domesticated.

"Are you making a side?" Camden's hands dug deep into the bowl of meat as he incorporated all his ingredients. I bit my lips and nodded, my thighs squeezed together in search of a small reprieve from what he caused. His eyes darkened. He'd noticed how turned on this was all making me. "What are you making?"

"Potato salad," I choked out and pushed away from the counter. Fuck, I needed to cool off. I opened the fridge door and prayed the cold air did just that. It took a moment as I tried to regulate my breathing. Camden unnerved me. Weakened my defenses.

I felt him behind me before he spoke. His body heat against my back seared me right through the thin cotton of my clothes. He was hard, throbbing against the flesh of my ass, and I couldn't help myself. Couldn't stop from pushing back and rubbing his hardness between my cheeks.

"I'd quit that if you want to eat tonight, *gatita*." His breath was hot against the back of my neck. I shivered, and a tiny mewl escaped me. "Have no problem fucking you right here. Fuck that, I'd take you against those balcony doors for all to see." The fingers of his right hand came around and cupped me. "Let them see my *gatita* purr for me. You'd like that, wouldn't you?"

"Yes." It was the truth. I'd let him without putting up any kind of fight.

"Good to know." He nipped my neck and then pulled slightly

back. "Get to work. I'm heading upstairs to the rooftop balcony to turn on the grill. Come up whenever you're ready." His fingers rubbed me twice, tight circles against my clit. My hand slammed down against his butcher block countertop. Small tremors rocked my body, and I started to gyrate against his hand.

The fingers against my clit disappeared and I ground my teeth in annoyance. Asshole.

"Get out," I spit out between clenched teeth. His laughter followed him out of the room and toward a set of stairs by the first bedroom on this floor. "Fucker," I mumbled under my breath and pulled out all the ingredients needed, and set to work.

Within ten minutes, I had everything cut and ready to mix. The potatoes were boiling and I was curious, so while they sat on high heat, I wandered around his home. Nothing too personal or intrusive, just looked at the pictures that sat on a table beside his leather sectional. One was of an older couple, both smiling at the camera with a cake in front of them. Another was of a woman in her forties hugging a tiny girl around the age of six. But none caught my eye like the one of him hugging a beautiful brunette to his body.

They were smiling and appeared happy. In love.

My chest ached. Who the hell was she?

"That would be Olivia," his voice whispered behind me, and I squeaked. When the hell had he come in? "That was on our wedding day, and the only reason it's still out, is because it's a reminder of what I became with her. What I never want to be again."

"You two made a stunning couple." It hurt me to the core to admit what was plain to see. His misery and coldness were caused by her treatment of him. Shaped him into what now stood behind me.

"She's my past."

"But where does your future lie?"

Silence filled the room. We didn't speak while I continued to look around at a part of him he never showed. His softer smiles threw me off and made me feel less secure. The water spilling over the rim of the pot on the stove pulled me away from him and the looming quiet that had descended upon us.

I set off to work in the kitchen and pushed away the sudden self-doubt that had bloomed in my chest. They'd looked so happy together—like everything that I wanted with him, but doubted he'd willingly give. Concentrating on the task at hand, I managed to put together the salad and a quick dessert of chocolate chip cookies. Nothing fancy, but I hoped he appreciated the effort.

I'd just set the cookies to cool when Camden came down the stairs. Sans shirt, he walked up to me and pushed me against the counter. Our chests pressed together, he tangled his long fingers into my hair and tipped my face up to look at him.

"Why are you hiding down here?" His kisses were a tease, soft and sweet. "Come upstairs." Like always, he didn't request. It was the mere formality of a command. "I think you'll enjoy my balcony. It's private, and I promise to misbehave."

A small giggle escaped my lips at his silliness. "Lead the way, massage boy."

The outdoor living space blew me away. We were at the very top floor of this condominium high-rise and with no one to spy on us. Total privacy. There was a small outdoor kitchen with a beautiful stainless grill, and beside that, a small sitting area. In one word —cozy.

"This is nice," I said admiringly and walked over to the covered hot tub. Not one part of me would have minded ending my night in there. Camden watched me as I explored his open space, his eyes darkening as I fingered the outside edge of the empty tub. "What a shame."

"Is it now?" His taunt made me laugh. "Why is it a shame?"

"Because the hot water on my naked flesh would have felt divine." Camden swallowed hard before making his way over to where I stood. His large hands framed my face, pulling me up to look at him before our lips touched.

Three times he pecked my lips before laying his forehead on

mine. "You have no idea of the craziness you cause inside of me. Turmoil and bliss."

"It's the same for me." I pulled his top lip between my lips and sucked, laving him with my tongue before pressing my teeth down. "You're driving me insane."

"Good." He smiled down at me and pushed a stray hair behind my ear. "Let's go eat, *gatita*. I brought you here for reasons other than making you scream my name."

"What reasons?"

"Enjoying your company. Getting to know you better. There are things I don't know, and I'm curious."

"Ask away," I said while pulling him toward the grill. The sizzling meat smelled amazing, and I unabashedly pointed to my stomach. "I'm starving. Put some food in me already."

He chuckled at my antics and checked the burgers on the grill. "They should be done in another five. How about we learn a little more about each other until then?"

"Like what?" Pulling one of the smaller chairs that surrounded a small bistro set near him, I sat down and waited for his answer. Camden bent at the waist and opened a small fridge, he pulled out two bottles and after popping the cap, offered me one.

"For one," he started and took a quick pull of his beer. "How old are you? I'm guessing early twenties, but I want specifics."

"Twenty-one and you?" Camden choked on his drink, his eyes wide. "Don't tell me you have an aversion to my age."

"No…" He coughed again and rubbed the back of his neck. "Just didn't know you were so fresh and innocent. It's having the opposite effect, really. I couldn't be harder for you if I tried. Legal and unblemished by society's bullshit."

"Good to know." I licked my lips and eyed him with hunger. "But I'm not that untouched and pure, Camden."

"One day that cute little mouth of yours will land you over my knee." The threat of a spanking wasn't a turn-off at all, and the flush over my cheeks told him so. "Bad *gatita,*" he admonished with a wink and pulled the burgers off the grill.

"Are you going to answer my question? How old are you?"

He continued to prepare our burgers with the works, and didn't spare me a single glance when he answered. "Thirty-two."

"Not surprised." His eyes snapped up at my words. "I've always been attracted to older men. Never dated one, but attracted nonetheless."

"Man, Amanda. Singular. Only me."

"Shut it, gramps." This caused him to laugh, almost dropping our food as he walked over to the small bistro table. He motioned for me to join him with a nod of his head. I liked this side of him. At ease and playful. Maybe, just maybe, Camden was opening up to me.

Maybe we'd be *more* sooner than I'd hoped.

"Are you going to tell me what that was between you two back there? What did you mean by the *real* reason he's here?"

He let out a humorless chuckle. "I've been waiting for you to bring that up."

"So?"

"Hunter came to my parents a few—"

I had to stop him there. "What do your parents have to do with this?"

"Look around, *Amanda.* How could a simple massage therapist be able to afford a penthouse in the middle of South Beach like this? Or any, for that matter?" He could see the confusion on my face, I was sure. Until now, I hadn't given much thought to how he acquired his place. Now, though, I needed to know. "My family owns the spa where I work. I'm actually the manager as well."

"This makes no sense, Camden." Things weren't adding up, like his story of struggling and working as maintenance while being married to Olivia. "Did you lie to me about—"

"No," he interrupted. "*Gatita*, my family believes in hard work and being independent. We aren't handed opportunities just because." Camden reached across the small table and took one of my hands in between his much larger ones. “Once married, I needed to maintain my family and work my way up to the position I hold. It's made me the man I am.”

Nodding, I grabbed my beer and took a long pull with my free hand. “So why are you a massage therapist? Why not just stay in management?”

“Simple. I love what I do.” His face was sincere and his tone honest.

“Okay, I believe you, but what about Hunter? How did he end up there?”

“His mother is a client,” he began, his fingers running soothing circles over the center of my palm. “She came in one day and overheard my mother and me talking about how much we needed another masseuse. Before we could finish, she’d jumped in and mentioned her son needing a job. That he would go to school and in the meantime. start doing the dirty work for free.”

“That makes no sense,” I interjected while serving us each a bit of the salad I had made. “Camden, that woman babies her son to the point of making him seem like an invalid. She’d never—”

“Well, she did.” Blunt and straight to the point was his answer. An answer that left me restless, while he took his time adding condiments to his burger.

“But why?” I asked. The silence and his patience were driving me up a wall.

“Because he’d gotten in trouble with the wrong crowd in New York, Mandi. She literally offered him up on a silver platter.” Camden watched me with troubled eyes as he filled me in, like he was scared and it made no sense. None of this did. “Hunter was flunking out of NYU and owed money to some unsavory people. A mixture of drugs and gambling were involved, and they pulled him out before the end result was worse than the money owed.”

Holy fuck. Then why was he so damned set on there being an us again?

He hadn’t come back for me.

"Did you want him too?" I looked up at Camden, not understanding his question. "You spoke your thoughts." A blush bloomed across my cheeks. "Do you want him back?"

"Hell, no." That answer appeased him, a small smile appearing on his handsome face. "I'm just trying to understand. We talked that night, you know? After I walked out on you at the sandwich shop, I went straight home, and he was there."

"Go on," he encouraged, and with the one hand not holding mine took a bite of his burger. I was mesmerized for a minute. The sensual way he swallowed did things to me. "Amanda." My eyes left his throat and settled on his eyes. "Continue."

Demanding fucker.

"Long story short, everyone argued and I took him outside. We fought, and he gave me some bullshit story on why he left. Asshole then proceeded to demand we continue from where we left off. I kicked him out not long after ripping him a new one."

A throaty chuckle escaped him before he kissed the tip of my fingers. "Good girl."

"It still doesn't answer why he wants me back."

"Yes, it does." I raised a brow in question. "He's trying to make everything as perfect as it once was. Get his parent's approval."

In other words, he was using me once again. *Fuck you, Hunter Knox.*

SEVENTEEN

Amanda

Camden had been absent from my life since the day of our dinner at his house.

No text. No call. No demands for my presence at our designated time.

I would have been worried if not for the spectacular memory of the time we had last week. He was attentive. Sweet. Talkative and open about more than just how good I felt wrapped around his cock.

"What time is your appointment today?" Courtney asked, bringing me back to the present. The girls and I had come to the school's gym to run a few drills. With summer winding down, our practices were starting back up. The competition was sure to be fierce this year, and we had a championship to defend.

"Not 'til three. Why?" She tossed me an unopened bottle of water. Twisting the top, I chugged half its contents before looking back at her. "What?"

"You still seeing him?" It was less of a question and more like a statement. Nodding, I tipped the bottle back and finished the rest. We'd just finished drills, and I was embarrassed to admit that I was a bit out of breath. "Are you two exclusive?"

How could I answer that question when I didn't know the answer myself? When I kissed him at the door that night, he was all smiles and soft touches. It seemed like we were heading in the monogamous direction.

"Something like that." It was the most truthful answer I could give her. "At least, I think we will be soon."

"Good enough." She took a drink of her own bottle and looked across the gym where some of the other girls were talking. "Hunter's been asking about you again," Courtney whispered so low I almost didn't hear her.

"Why can't he just let me be?" It was rhetorical. I'd told her everything Camden had shared with me, and to say she was livid would be putting it mildly.

"Because he's a selfish mommy's boy who's been put in a time out." The entire situation was insane and fucked up on so many levels, but funny at the same time. I couldn't hold in the giggle that escaped even if I tried. "He's looking to get off for good behavior and you are exactly what his parents want."

"Where do you get that from?"

Turning to face me, she squeezed my shoulder and gave me a sad smile. "I overheard them talking a few days ago—his mom and ours. I'd just happen to come downstairs when Susana agreed with his mom, saying you both were so good together. How it's only a matter of time before you gave in and came to your senses."

"Well, they can keep on dreaming. It isn't going to happen." *You have got to be kidding me!* Mom promised she'd butt out. Hunter and I will never be again.

"I know that, Mandi. Just thought you should know what's going on." And I appreciated it. Courtney always had my back and I, hers. Pulling her in for a hug, I squeezed her tight and kissed her cheek.

"Thank you." She waved me off and opened her mouth to speak when my phone rang, cutting her off. It was Camden's tone, the one I'd given him the same night I left his house.

Courtney rolled her eyes and walked toward Jennifer and Steph. They were busy having a three-point shoot-off.

"Hello."

"Amanda?" His breathing was a bit loud, as if he'd been running around. It also caught me off guard that he used my first name. Since when was I Amanda to him?

Stop it. He's probably at work and trying to be professional, I mentally chastised myself.

"Hey, Camden. I swear I'll be on time." He didn't laugh. Didn't react. "Is everything okay?"

"Yeah…" He cleared his throat before continuing. "Listen, I have to cancel today's appointment. Something's come up, and I need to leave within the next few minutes. Sorry." His tone was cold. Detached. Something wasn't right, I felt this in the way my chest tightened.

Pushing back the looming dread I felt, I took in a deep breath and tried to center myself. "Is everything okay? Can I help—"

"No," he hissed and then muttered something underneath his breath. "I don't need your help, Amanda. Everything will be fine, okay? We'll reschedule once I'm back."

"Okay." What else was there to say? *No, don't go. I need you.* It was apparent by his abrupt behavior that he was in a hurry, and I didn't want to delay him. "Don't worry, Camden. I'll see you—" He hung up before I finished.

I don't know how long I stood staring at my phone trying to decipher just what had happened. How it had all gone wrong. Was this his way of blowing me off?

Couldn't be. Maybe I was making this a bigger deal than it was. He would be back and explain. People act very differently when faced with emergency situations. Yes, that had to be it.

"You okay, Mandi?" Steph called out from across the court. Was I? I didn't know.

"I'm fine, just received a weird phone call." Her brow rose in question while the other two looked on with interest. "He canceled our appointment. Something about an emergency and having to leave."

"Okay. Shit happens." That was Jennifer adding in her two cents. Always blunt. Sighing, I put my phone back in the pocket of my bag and walked to center court with them. The way he hung up was rubbing me the wrong way, and I needed to distract myself before my thoughts went down a dark hole.

"I know that…it's the way he spoke. In a rush, and cold."

Jennifer shrugged and dribbled the ball in her hand. "He isn't Hunter, and you're overthinking this." She pulled her arms up and back before flicking her wrist and letting the ball go. It was all net. "Why don't we all head to Rage tonight? It's been a while, and I could use a night out with my girls."

"Everything okay with you?" I asked her.

She shrugged and looked over at our coach. The man wasn't supposed to be at this drill but had shown up anyway. We knew why he was here and watched on with amusement as his eyes would wander over to Jennifer every few minutes.

"Jennifer," Court giggled and smacked her in the ass, "pay attention, you whore."

"What?" Her angry hiss was met with our laughter.

"Never mind." Courtney turned back toward Steph and me. "We doing Rage or what?"

"I'm in," Stephanie chimed, taking her post to release her next shot.

"Me too." There wasn't anything better for me to do today, and I refused to stay home and dwell. The uncertainty and doubt would drive me insane. I'd think of only the worst and ruin what we could have. "Let's meet at ten by the doors?" The girls all nodded, and practice continued. I had a good feeling tonight would be just what I needed to get over my funk.

~

RAGE WAS PACKED TONIGHT, MORE SO THAN I WOULD'VE EXPECTED for a Wednesday night. House music blared from the speakers and the dance floor was jammed with people dancing, hands thrown up in the air and gyrating to the beat.

The girls and I didn't feel like getting too dressed up tonight and all settled for tight skinny jeans and all-too-tight tank tops. Mine was special to me. It was one I pilfered from my mom's closet a year ago. Her fascination with 80s' metal hair bands was a secret amongst her friends, but not me or Dad. She loved Guns N' Roses, and at their Use Your Illusion tour, she bought the shirt I wore.

"Who's heading to the bar?" Jennifer yelled over the music. We were standing just inside the door and trying to come up with a plan. Two would get the first round, and the others would score a table.

"I'll head to the bar…the usual?" I asked them, and after their nod of confirmation, I pulled a dancing Stephanie with me. "God, I needed this."

"We all did." Boy was her statement the truth. Practice today was brutal. In our Coach's eyes, we'd become out of shape in the last few weeks. How that happened within two months beats me, but if the way we were gulping in air after a simple scrimmage was anything to go by…we were screwed. "My ass hurts."

Laughter bubbled up inside of me and I giggled. "Your ass, my pussy." She laughed right along with me, remembering the awkward split I landed in when I tripped during a play. Finally, the bar was in our sights, and my mouth watered.

I deserved my screwdriver. We were a few feet away when someone grabbed me by the elbow, stopping me in my tracks. The hairs on the back of my neck stood on end. I knew this person—of that, there was no doubt. Problem was, their touch wasn't welcomed.

"Are you following me, Hunter?" The iciness in my tone didn't stop him from pulling me in just a tiny bit closer. From him sniffing my hair."Get off!"

"Fuck, you look beautiful."

"If you don't let me go—"

"Is it all for *him*?" He spat the last word; the fingers on my arm tightening, and I winced. "Is it?"

"What are you talking about? You need to stop this."

Stephanie put a hand between us, trying to separate us, but he wouldn't budge. He looked smug. The look on his face was one of a person gloating.

"Dude, you need to back off. She's made it clear that she doesn't want you." Stephanie pushed again to no avail. I raised my leg, dead set on kneeing him, when he abruptly pulled my face—forced my attention on a table to my right.

At first, I didn't know what I was supposed to be looking at. But then, it all made sense, and the pain that wracked my body could only be described as acid being poured on an open wound. My eyes couldn't pull themselves away.

How? Why?

"You didn't know…did you?" Hunter whispered low, remorse now coloring his tone. His shoulders slumped and his arm loosened its hold. "Fuck. Shit, Mandi. I swear I thought you were here together and he was being, well, him. All I wanted was for you to see that I was better."

"What the fuck are you talking about, Hunter? Why is she trembling?" Steph's words didn't register. Nothing did.

Camden was a few feet away from me—with her. Cynthia was beside him at a small table with another couple. Laughing. Drinking. I watched as she leaned against his broad chest and he put his arm around her.

Watched as she kissed his jaw, and he let her.

A sob ripped itself from me, and my knees weakened. Almost as if he had somehow heard the sound, Camden's eyes snapped up and landed on mine. In those swirling waters was guilt, and it was more than I could take. My hand reached out and fisted Hunter's shirt, using it as a shield for all the hurt and rejection that filled me.

Camden's eyes followed the movement and narrowed. He made a

move to stand up, but Cynthia pulled him down and nuzzled his chest. Again, he let her. Even pulled her closer.

"Get me out of here," I whispered into Hunter's shirt. His arms snaked around my waist and hugged me.

"That's Camden," Hunter said to Stephanie, pointing over at the angry man that just broke my heart. The same man who was now watching our interactions with undisguised ire.

"That motherfucker!" she screeched and turned to make her way to him. I stopped her before she could. It wasn't worth it. Not anymore. Done. This was the final drop of water to what was an already full cup. "Why are you stopping me? He's an asshole and deserves everything I have to say and more."

"Won't solve a thing. Just get me out of here." Couldn't they hear the desperation in my voice?

"No." Hunter's anger caused me to recoil away. "Sorry, babe. I'm not trying to be a bigger dick than I've already been." His hands reached out for mine, and this time I let him take them. "I get it now. You don't love me, and as much as it hurts my pride, I do get it."

"Huh?" I'm sorry, but now was just not the time to discuss shit that made no sense.

"You never cried like this when I told you I was leaving, that we were done. Yet for him, you tremble in anguish."

"Hunter, I—"

"Shhh…" He placed a finger over my lips. "I'm not saying this because I need leverage over you."

Stephanie snorted beside us. "Sorry, Knox, but I don't buy it."

"And I don't need you to," he growled. "I've made a lot of mistakes and I'm not proud of how I've handled things, but rejection is something I don't handle well. Look, Mandi, I'm sorry." Nodding, I looked away from him and over to Camden. His eyes were narrowed, those glorious lips set in a hard line. Tears continued to fall from my face, and he noticed this.

The harshness disappeared, and now remorse shined in those beautiful orbs. I watched transfixed, as he pushed her hand away and stood. Cynthia called his name, grabbed his hand, but he was determined to get to me.

Without losing sight of him, I pulled Hunter down to my level. "Let's dance."

"Mandi, I know that—"

"He's coming over here, you idiot," I whispered harshly. "There's no way in hell I can face him right now. I'm an angry, emotional mess and need to get away." Camden was a few feet away now, his eyes boring into mine. *Fuck, no. Right now, I can't deal with him.* "Please."

The pure fright and desperation in my voice jolted Hunter into action, and right before Camden reached us, I was pulled away to dance. Our eyes never lost sight of the other.

He mouthed the words "let's talk," but I shook my head. His shoulders slumped, his posture defeated.

Stephanie stood with Courtney and Jennifer beside him, each of their faces pinched in anger. They eyed him with disdain and me with pity. I didn't want their goddamned pity.

"Can we go?" My throat felt raw and my eyes stung.

"Is that what you want, Amanda?" Hunter ran the back of his fingers up and down my back in a soothing action. It didn't work; it made it worse. His touch wasn't the one I needed to make things better. "I'll keep him away so you can hang out with the girls."

Nodding, I laid my head on his chest and closed my eyes. "I need to get out of here."

Hunter kissed the top of my head before releasing me and signaling the girls over. Their conversation was nothing more than a dull whisper in the background. If they argued or killed each other at that moment, I didn't care.

I looked over at Camden one last time, and the resignation in his eyes almost made me crumble.

This was the end of whatever I thought we had.

Book #2: Taunting Lips is out NOW!!!
Read the second part to this delicious duet today.
Happy Reading!!!

Buy Link:
https://books2read.com/u/4jDlqj

About The Author

Elena M. Reyes is the epitome of a Floridian and if she could live in her beloved flip-flops, she would.

As a small child, she was always intrigued by all forms of art: whether it was dancing to island rhythms, or painting with any medium she could get her hands on. Her passion for reading over the years has amassed her with hours of pleasure, but it wasn't until she stumbled upon fanfiction that her thirst to write overtook her world.

She's a short and sassy Latina with an adorable pup, a kiddo that keeps her on her toes, and a husband who claims she'll cause him to go bald prematurely. Lol

EMAIL: REYES139FF@GMAIL.COM

Elena's Marked Girls.

Come join the naughty fun.
Link: https://www.facebook.com/groups/1710869452526025/

NEWSLETTER SIGNUP:
http://bit.ly/2nHJxTI

facebook.com/AuthorElenaMReyes
twitter.com/ElenaMReyes
instagram.com/elenar139
tiktok.com/@elenamreyes?
bookbub.com/authors/elena-m-reyes
amazon.com/Elena-M-Reyes/e/B00E3E26X8/ref=dp_byline_cont_pop_ebooks_1

Also by Elena M. Reyes

ALSO, BY ELENA M. REYES

SERIES:

FATE'S BITE SERIES

LITTLE LIES

LITTLE MATE

HALF TRUTHS {COMING 2022)

OMISSION {TBD}

SERIES:

BEAUTIFUL SINNER SERIES

Each book is a standalone.

Now Live!

SIN (#1)

COVET (#2)

MINE (#3)

YOURS (#4)

RISQUE #5

Beautiful Sinner Spin-Off

CORRUPT

(Marked Series)

Marking Her #1

Marking Him #2

Scars #2.5

Marked #3

(I Saw You)

I Saw You

I Love You #1.5

Teasing Hands Duet

Teasing Hands #1

Taunting Lips #2

SAFE ROMANCE:

Taste Of You

Doctor's Orders

Back To You

STANDALONES:

Craving Sugar

Stolen Kisses

www.ingramcontent.com/pod-product-compliance
Ingram Content Group UK Ltd.
Pitfield, Milton Keynes, MK11 3LW, UK
UKHW042017190726
13854UKWH00005B/2337

9 798401 959041